DRAGON DADDY'S NANNY

MISTY VALE SHIFTERS 1

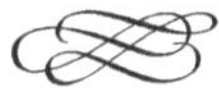

SAMANTHA LEAL

Dragon Daddy's Nanny

Copyright ©2020 by Samantha Leal

https://www.totallyromancebooks.com/samantha-leal

Join the Totally Romance Facebook Group!

CONTENTS

CHAPTER 1

"Okay, so I guess this is how it's done in all the great romance novels!" Amelia said with a grin as she let her finger hover over the map, willing her subconscious to find somewhere spectacular.

When she brought her hand down and she felt her fingertip connect with the smooth paper underneath, her heart skipped a beat and her skin tingled with anticipation.

This was it.

She eased her eyes open slowly, her vision adjusting to the myriad of lines all coming together into one spot where she had randomly placed her forefinger, a place in time and space that was surely about to change her life. And yet, it was somewhere she didn't even yet know.

When she focused and the words came popping out at her, she instinctively found herself smiling.

Misty Vale.

From what she could tell from the map, it appeared to be a little town nestled in the Rockies, somewhere she had never ventured before in her life, but she supposed some-where that had also always intrigued her. It would certainly be a lot different to here. She had lived by the beach her entire life. But it's not as if that had worked out so well for her.

"Misty Vale." She said it aloud and let it roll around on her tongue. Her soul liked it. It sounded good. Wholesome. Somewhere that would surely bring her more happiness than here. Somewhere that could give her hope.

Without wasting a moment longer, she jumped to her feet and sprang into action. Today was the day she was going to change her life.

* * *

WITH HER PACK HITCHED HIGH ON HER SHOULDER AND WITH A spring in her step, Amelia couldn't help but grin from ear to ear. The cold, crisp air, the scent of pine and the beautiful fall leaves were the first thing that struck her as she walked into town on her first day and saw how picturesque and stunning Misty Vale was. Being a beach girl for as long as she had known, it was certainly going to be a different way of life out here in her new town. She was in awe at how beautiful it was, and as she wandered around taking it all in, she knew she had found somewhere special. It was the perfect place to begin again and to forget her past and all the trouble that had gone along with it.

It was the kind of town you saw in the movies, one that Amelia had barely even dared think existed until she had played roulette with the map a few days before. She looked up and saw The Grand Lodge was sitting on the mountain, looking down over the town as if it were some kind of over-seer, and it made her think again of places she had seen on TV. Like some perfect little place off the beaten track in countries like Switzerland, its colors popping out of the landscape, adding to the reds and greens, and giving the mountainside a festive feel. She began to walk and explore, and Main Street was long and full of incredible shops. She smiled as she spotted a cute little candy store, a beautician, gift shops and bars that were all independent and quirky in their own way. She didn't think she had yet to see a chain store or big corporation, and as she ventured further into this lovely little place, she found herself feeling right at home. Something that kept appearing was an image that must be the town's crest. There was a castle in the middle of it with a crown hovering overhead, and an ancient-looking dragon on one side and what she thought may have been a bear on the other. It looked like something from the Scottish Highlands, old and powerful, but it made her smile.

Amelia stopped when she reached a B&B and hitched her bag back onto her shoulder. It had been a long train ride and she was aching and tired. All she could think about was sleep, but she needed somewhere to crash and ditch her things before she headed out to look for a job, and she wasn't going to waste any time doing it.

She reached for the doors of the B&B at the exact same time that they swung open, and she felt the unwelcome thud of the door hitting her shoulder as her bag went crashing to the ground.

"Ouch," she whispered as she tried to regain her composure, and she instinctively bent down to collect her things. She was aware of someone bending down too, and as she looked up, she saw him, right there in front of her eyes, looking back at her with disdain.

"I'm sorry," he said with a raised brow. "I almost took you out there."

Amelia found herself scowling, but at the same time, her heart faltered for a moment as she took in the tall dark guy with broad shoulders, a black beard, and a smoldering stare. Man, he was hot. Clearly trouble, but hot. He was dressed casually, in a pair of dark blue jeans and a black sweatshirt, but she could tell that his clothes weren't just from any old store. They looked well-made and expensive. His eyes were heavy and brooding, and as they rested briefly on hers again, she felt stunned into stillness.

Wow...

That was the only thought that went through her mind as she found herself kneeling there as if she had been frozen to the ground.

"I... well, thanks, I guess..." she said, trying to mimic his manor.

He scooped up her bag and smiled sheepishly as they both rose to their feet. She couldn't tell why, but the way he was looking at her was as if she had done something wrong and he was trying to figure her out. As if he wanted to ask her what the hell she had been doing there.

"Should watch where you're going next time," he said with amusement and then he winked, and it made her skin tingle.

He was so handsome, so intimidating in his stance and the way he held himself. He was like no one she had ever seen before; someone so confident in their own skin, someone who seemed to command attention. It was as if the whole of Main Street had stopped when he had stepped outside, and yet, here she was, caught in his glare and feeling as if he was seeing deep into her soul. Her skin burned with something she could only liken to intense excitement, and she suddenly became aware that her mouth must have been gaping open and she closed it tight. He seemed to narrow his eyes at her, as if he were sizing her up again, but he smiled warmly. She gave a weak smile and went to ask him if he made a habit of almost knocking girls out with swing doors, but before she had chance, he took another step, and he was moving away, glancing back over his shoulder at her as he made his way down Main Street in the direction of the mountain.

Amelia faltered for a moment, unsure of what had just happened. She felt stunned. Shaken. Her heart was pounding slightly, and she felt in a daze. It was obviously just an accident, a silly little moment of oversite. But had he been rude? Or had she been acting dumb because he was so goddam good-looking? She shook her head and laughed to herself. She was such a ditz! If she was going to make it in a new town, she was going to have to play it cooler than that when a handsome guy appeared in front of her. Plus, that most certainly was not what she was about anymore, anyway. Men were the last thing on her mind after the year she'd had. She shook the thoughts away, not letting herself go there. She absolutely would not let the events of her past ruin what was supposed to be her new beginning.

She felt as if she still had his eyes on her, and she found herself looking ahead to see if he was still walking down Main Street, but the crowd had surged outside one of the coffee houses and he was gone. She sighed and pushed open the door to the B&B and headed inside, still feeling as if her feathers had been slightly ruffled and she needed to prune them back into their glorious self.

After checking in and finding her room, she threw her bags down on the floor and flopped down on the bed, stretching her arms high over her head and enjoying the feel of finally being off her feet and somewhere cozy and warm. This was it. This, as they say, was the first day of the rest of her life.

She hugged her arms around herself and closed her eyes. It had been a rough year, with lots of setbacks and plenty to run away from. But she had done it. She had packed up and fled, and now she was somewhere new, somewhere that filled her with hope, and somewhere she could finally let the memories of her relationship with Toby disappear. There was nothing here in Misty Vale to remind her of what had happened between them. Nothing that would evoke a feeling or strong memory when she stepped inside a restaurant or a store. And she had done the ultimate thing to make sure she never suffered at the hands of someone like him again, she had done what he always tried to tell her she couldn't do. She had gone out on her own and she was being independent. She didn't need someone to guide her, and she certainly didn't need to be under anyone else's control. She was her own woman, she was regaining her life, and she was starting again, without someone trying to erase who she truly was so that she fit their perfect image.

She smiled to herself knowingly and felt a surge of pride again. She really was going to live now. The past was long dead, and she was ready for her future.

CHAPTER 2

As Dash walked down Main Street, he had to fight every urge inside of him not to turn back and stare at the beautiful woman who he had just bumped into outside of the B&B. Misty Vale hadn't thrown him any surprises in a long time, but something about her had intrigued him, and he was already worried what that something may be.

After the experience with women he'd had, the last thing he wanted was to find his inner beast stirred by a cute little stranger.

Not on his life.

"Hi, Dash," old Mrs. Brown called from across the street outside the small café where the older generation of town met every week to crochet and swap stories. Dash smiled and raised his hand, waving back to her and her group of friends, all looking very at home there, sipping cups of coffee and talking about the good old days.

He always wondered what it must have been like for them, growing up in Misty Vale in a much simpler time before years of animosity had changed things. But in a way, he was glad that he didn't know, it would surely only make him sad that he and his daughter wouldn't have the same luxury of feeling like all was right with the world.

He reached into his pocket for the keys to his truck and when he opened the door and climbed inside, he looked in the rearview mirror and noticed the red tint to his cheeks. His heart was running away beneath his skin and his dragon was stirring.

That woman… she really had done something to him. And from only one run-in. The tiniest patch in time, brought on by complete coincidence, and yet, now she was in his head. He furrowed his brow and started the engine. He didn't have time for distractions today; he had a child to collect and a problem to solve as soon as possible. His inner demons were going to have to wait.

He pulled into traffic and the hustle and bustle of Main Street with his music blaring, and he tapped the wheel and sang along as he made his way to school. He felt good, all things considered. And now, he couldn't wait to see Nora and give her the biggest hug and chat about her day.

* * *

"DADDY!" SHE BEAMED AS SHE RAN DOWN THE SCHOOL STEPS and flung her arms around his neck, kissing him on the cheek as he breathed her in and held her tight.

These were the moments he lived for, they were the ones that made everything worthwhile. The past may have been hard, and they may have overcome a lot to get there, but he and his daughter were happy and settled, and she came before anything else.

"How was your day, sweetheart?" he asked as they drove back along Main Street and he found his eyes instinctively scanning the spot outside the B&B where he had collided with the cute stranger only an hour before.

8

"It was fun," Nora giggled. "We learned all about the planets, we looked at pictures of Earth and Mars."

"Wow," Dash laughed. "That sounds pretty exciting."

"It was," Nora said thoughtfully. "I like Earth the best... because that's where we live."

He reached over and ruffled her hair, feeling a great sense of relief and pride. He hadn't done so bad when it came to raising her. He was proud of the lovely girl she was becoming.

He slowed his truck and pulled into a parking spot close to one of his offices and shut off the engine. Nora was smiling happily, looking out the window and waited patiently for him to come around to her side to unbuckle her and let her out. This was just part of their everyday routine now; afterschool pickups usually consisted of visiting the office for at least an hour to make sure everything was in order. But Dash longed to be able to give Nora a bit more normality. He felt bad that she had to spend her free time sitting around in the office when she could be doing afterschool classes or at Kid's Club up at the golf resort. Even the thought of her settling in at home, doing her homework and waiting for her dinner to be made stirred something in him, and it made his guilt rise. A five-year-old shouldn't have to be constantly hanging around her father's place of business, but what choice did he have?

It's time you got a proper nanny, he thought.

He had been thinking it for some time now, and it was something he definitely wanted to explore, but so far, all of the agencies he had tried hadn't come up with someone quite special enough to be the right person to spend so much time with Nora. She hadn't bonded with anyone, and she hadn't wanted them to come again. It was hard, because all Dash wanted was to make her happy and know that she was with someone he could trust, and she adored.

He walked through the office doors and watched as Nora bounced onto the black plush velvet couch that sat proudly in the front window and looked up at the flatscreen TV ahead, showing the business news on a national channel. Dash checked his watch. The office was open for a couple more hours and he knew it was unlikely that any clients would be coming in this late in the day. He reached for the remote, which was hidden in the chest of drawers below the TV and flicked it to a kids' show.

"There you go, sweetheart," he said. "I'll be as quick as I can, then we just need to run down the street to do one more building check."

Nora nodded at him obediently, and he smiled.

He really was the luckiest guy in the world.

CHAPTER 3

*O*ktoberfest.

The words were printed big and bold on the huge banner that hung across the very center of Main Street, adorned with twinkling lights that were already sparkling even when the sun had yet to fully set.

Fall was starting to kick in, and Misty Vale clearly was ready to embrace it. The leaves on the trees were becoming a beautiful orange, and the days were becoming much shorter. Amelia looked at the big clock sitting proud on the town hall building and she could see that it was getting close to 6pm. It had been a wild day for her, coming to a new place and trying to find her bearings, but after an initial rest, followed by a couple of hours of exploring, she was starting to feel as if this place was starting to feel more like home.

She had spoken to the lady at the reception of the B&B and asked her where the best place to look for work was and she had told her to find the noticeboards at the Town Hall. Back in her hometown, Amelia had worked in childcare, babysitting as much as possible, since she was young, and eventually, moved on to school and nursery settings. Since she had met Toby, her career had taken a backseat, and now she felt a little lost. She had been out of work for so long, almost two years, but she was desperate to get back to doing something she loved. Toby had done his best to make sure she didn't have too much of a life outside of him, and work had been the first thing to go. Her mom had only made the problem worse by telling her it was up to Amelia to make sure her man was happy and never lost interest. She should follow his wishes and forget about work for a while, dress right, make an effort with her appearance, always be done up appropriately and not let standards slip. It had made her so anxious, and the thought of ever finding a job again without having to look over her shoulder had become too hard back home. So, with Toby firmly in the past, she had left. Now, she was out in the world on her own again and she was ready to reclaim her life.

She wandered along Main Street and took in all the lovely little stores. They were all done up for Fall, bursting with color in the windows, reds and oranges, twinkling lights, pumpkins and apples. She smiled as she looked at the display in the book store and scanned the rest of the window for the site of any little signs that may indicate they were looking for extra staff now that the holidays were fast approaching, and by the looks of things, an Oktoberfest was coming to town, which would, no doubt, see an influx of visitors.

She carried on walking when the beauticians caught her eye. She turned and looked at her reflection in the mirror and reached up and looked at her split ends. It had been quite a while since she had bothered with her hair or nails or anything like that. Almost in rebellion, but she felt the need to reinvent herself slightly and do a little pampering while she was at it. She shrugged, smiled, and made her way over. She may as well strike while the iron was hot!

"Hello and welcome to Jane's," a very smiley girl said

when she walked through the door. She had bright, lovely, almond eyes and long, chocolatey hair. She looked as if she were a similar age to Amelia, and she exuded confidence and kindness.

"Hello," Amelia smiled.

Jane stepped out from behind the counter and walked over, and Amelia found herself looking around at the nail bars and make up stations, the chairs and mirrors, and the hair color charts and washers and dryers.

"How can I help?" the girl smiled.

"Well," Amelia began. "I'm not really all that sure. I'm new in town, and I'm looking for work, but also, I'm hoping to get a bit of a makeover, and wondering if I could be booked in?"

"Oh, wonderful," the girl said as she held out her hand, and Amelia reached and shook it. "I'm Jane, and this is my salon."

"Amelia," she smiled.

"So, you're new in town?" Jane asked. "What brings you to little old Misty Vale? Are you extending a vacation?"

"Actually, no…" Amelia half laughed. "It's a bit of a crazy story, but I just did the old finger on the map trick, and here I am. Fresh start required, and looking to settle somewhere new."

"Oh, I love that!" Jane beamed as she clapped her hands together. "I'm jealous, I always daydreamed about doing something similar myself."

"Well, I don't know why you would ever want to leave somewhere like here," Amelia said honestly. "It's just wonderful, I've never been anywhere like it."

"It is pretty special, I suppose," Jane agreed. "I think I probably take it for granted because I'm so used to it!"

"That's always the way," Amelia smiled.

"Well, I can't help you out on the work front," Jane said. "I'm kind of a one-man band here, at the moment, with some girls who rent chairs and spaces from me on certain days of the week, but I can help you with the makeover!" She winked and stepped back toward the main desk and reached for a big, hardbacked diary and began flicking through some very full-looking pages.

"The rest of this week is pretty mega," she said. "But I'd love to help a girl out, so I can stay open a little later for you, if that works?"

Amelia couldn't believe her luck.

"That would be amazing," she smiled.

"Sure," Jane said as she picked up her pen and clicked the top. "How about the day after tomorrow?"

Amelia nodded, almost stunned. Things couldn't be working out any better on her first day in town. She had clocked a rather handsome guy, had found somewhere to stay that wasn't going to cost her the Earth, already felt like she was making a friend, and had her first plans set in stone for a couple of days' time where she could focus even more on her reinvention.

"Perfect," Jane said as she scribbled Amelia's name down in the diary. "If you get here around 5pm, then we will have plenty of time to do whatever you like."

"I'll have a think and try to be prepared," Amelia laughed.

Jane winked and as Amelia headed for the door, she felt a warm and fuzzy feeling inside.

She was beginning to like Misty Vale a lot.

* * *

THE DOORS TO THE B&B REFLECTED THE LIGHTS FROM THE rest of the town as she headed back toward them as darkness had descended. She had walked for a little longer, looking in various windows and asking at a few counters to see if anyone knew of any job openings. She hadn't had much luck so far, but someone had told her there was a job board close to the town hall, and she vowed to make it her first port of call in the morning, after she had gotten some much deserved rest.

As she stepped through the doors and into the warm and welcoming lobby of the B&B, the first thing she heard was the familiar sound of Maude, the little lady at the check-in desk, as she laughed and then said, "Oh look, here she is now."

Amelia looked up to see her speaking with a man who had his back to her, but as he began to turn and look over his shoulder, Amelia couldn't believe that it was actually him...

The man from earlier, the one who had accidentally pushed the door into her and then looked at her as if she were crazy while he helped her pick up her bags.

Amelia's heart pounded harder in her chest, and she felt her face flare red.

Oh shit, she thought. Don't embarrass yourself again.

She stopped in her tracks and felt his eyes on her. The way he was looking at her was with slight amusement again, but this time, his eyes were kinder and it made her feel slightly more at ease, even if she couldn't tell if she were being lured into some kind of hot man trap or not. She paused and waited.

"Amelia, dear," the lady at the desk said. "We were just talking about you."

"I thought my ears were burning," she half laughed, hoping from the very bottom of her soul that she wasn't blushing too badly. She didn't know why, but she felt as if she had just wandered into the lion's den. The hot guy was staring at her as if she were some kind of prey and he was ready to pounce, and it was making her all kinds of nervous and shy.

"All good, I hope?" Amelia said to divert attention away

from the fact she was nervously fidgeting. His eyes had yet to move, and she could sense the deepness of them. He was looking at her with intrigue and was doing more than sizing her up this time.

What the hell had they been talking about?

"I was just telling Mr. Livingstone that you could very well be the answer to all of his problems."

The context of the words and how she was feeling took her by surprise and she gulped.

"I could?" she asked with a wry smile, raising her eyebrow.

Luckily, his dark and controlled façade seemed to crack slightly, and he smiled properly, this time, laughing and looking back at Maude with affection.

"Maude really does have a way with words," he mused.

He stepped forward and held out his hand. As he got closer, Amelia was sure she could feel a heat between them, something that kept rising and made the skin on her chest flame even harder. She was glad she was wearing a high-neck sweater, or she was sure he would be able to see her slowly turning the color of a tomato from her toes right up to the top of her head.

"Nice to meet you," he said, and then after a pause and with much emphasis… *"Again."*

She smiled meekly and let her hand softly slide into his. When he gripped hers and they shook, she felt a powerful jolt and it made her gasp. His eyes didn't move from her, but instead, he blinked and breathed in deep. Again, it was controlled, as if he had almost been expecting it but maybe not as intense. He breathed deeply out of his nose and then their hands slowly broke apart.

"I'm Amelia," she managed to croak, her throat suddenly dry and her nerves overpowering.

"Mr. Livingstone," he smiled as he looked back over his

shoulder at Maude at the desk. "But as I keep insisting to my friend here, please, do call me Dash."

Dash.

Wow.

Amelia swallowed and felt the need to fan her face with both hands, but she kept herself under control.

"Daddy!" a little voice came bouncing into the room from off in one of the halls, quickly followed by a set of footsteps, and then, a little girl emerged, looking rosy-cheeked and very pleased with herself. Amelia couldn't help but smile and her eyes lit up.

She was adorable, and as she ran toward Dash and wrapped her arms around his legs, she could see the resemblance immediately.

"Hello there," Amelia beamed as she looked down at the little girl, her big wide eyes staring up at her.

"Hello," she said back, very politely. "My name is Nora."

"And I'm Amelia, how do you do?" she said in her best Mary Poppins accent.

"She's like Mary Poppins, Daddy," Nora smiled, getting the reference immediately. "It's one of my favorite films."

"She sounds like a real-life Mary Poppins to me too," Maude said. "From what we were talking about earlier."

She nodded at Amelia and then at Dash, as if urging them onto a specific conversation.

"Ah, yes," Dash smiled knowingly. "I was just chatting with Maude here about how we need someone to help out with Nora… so I don't have to keep dragging her to business meetings after school. And she said it was a coincidence, but she had just met the most wonderful woman, today, who was new in town, and was looking for work, with plenty of experience in childcare."

Amelia smiled and brushed a strand of hair behind her ear.

"And then you appeared, as if by magic," Dash said. His gaze still firmly fixed on her, taking her in and making her even more nervous, if that was at all possible.

"Thank you, Maude," she smiled. "That's very kind of you to mention me."

Maude cocked her head to the side and then started to busy herself behind the counter as if she were checking out of the conversation and leaving them to it.

Dash smiled and looked down at Nora and then back to Amelia again.

"Maybe we could have a chat?" he asked.

Amelia nodded, her mouth suddenly ceasing to work again.

"I can't hang around now, as it's getting late and Nora needs to be home for her dinner and bath, but how about tomorrow? Will you be around town?"

"Sure," Amelia smiled. "I could meet you late morning?"

He nodded and then paused for a moment.

"Do you know of the coffee house across the street? Misty Brews?"

Amelia was sure she had seen it.

"I sure do," she smiled.

"I'll catch you there around eleven?"

"Perfect," Amelia said.

"And I will need to see some checkable references, as well as an up-to-date resume."

"No problem," Amelia said. Luckily, knowing she would be looking for work in her new town, she had updated her resume and had plenty of copies ready to go.

"Well, then," he said as he took hold of Nora's hand before his eyes fell on Amelia's again. "I will see you tomorrow."

"See you tomorrow," Amelia managed to say. "And it was lovely to meet you, Nora."

"And you, Mary Poppins," Nora said cheekily.

Amelia and Dash both laughed, and then, she watched as they made their way to the doors and Dash cast back a lingering glance at her.

Wow. Wow. Wow.

What the fuck had just happened?

Amelia didn't have a clue, but she couldn't help but feel as if it were something powerful and possibly verging on fate.

When Dash and Nora were out of sight, she finally took the deep breath she had been waiting to take, and she felt the blood rush back to her head after it had worked its way fully to her crazily beating heart.

Dash Livingstone… who and what are you? she thought.

All she knew was that she couldn't wait to find out.

CHAPTER 4

*M*isty Brews had been sitting pretty in the middle of Main Street for the past couple of years and had gone from one success to another. Dash had been involved in the acquisition of the building almost a decade earlier, after the original owner had died, and he had loved seeing it being taken over and turned into something positive for the town. He and his family owned a lot of property and knew what they were doing when it came to making a buck or two. The Livingstone's had been in Misty Vale since the first settlers had arrived, and they had made a lot of good decisions, which had ensured they had risen to the very top when it came to the inner workings of the town. They had even played a part in The Grand Lodge being built way back at the turn of the century and had seen their business empire grow and increase with success. But all of this meant that Dash was one very busy man… and he had Nora to think about. He couldn't be in two places at once, and with Nora's mother no longer being a part of their lives, he had to do something about it, so he could give his daughter a more normal life.

After all of these years, it wasn't often that Nora's mother popped into his head after all that had happened between them. But when it came to things like this, he couldn't help but wonder what she was doing and where she was. The last he had heard, she was partying her way across Europe and had married a wealthy man over there. She was well out of his and Nora's life, and Dash was glad. But the pang of anger for her still lingered when he thought of what Nora had been denied. He had no idea how a mother could walk away from her child. And he would never understand it. He was just glad that they had thrived, just the two of them, that he had grown well in his role of a single father, and it was only now that he truly felt the need for any kind of assistance. Nora had passions that she wanted to explore outside of school, she loved Kid's Club up at the golf resort, and she had regularly talked about starting dance lessons, but with the demands of Dash's business, and the extent of which he needed to be present, he couldn't indulge her and keep his head above water with work. It just wasn't possible, even if it broke his heart to hand the reins over to someone else temporarily.

He wandered inside the doors to the coffee house and looked around. As usual, it was warm and welcoming inside, with a large, open, roaring fire, soft music playing in the background, big, comfy couches nestled in the alcoves and a selection of tables to choose from in the center of the room. He made his way to the counter and smiled at the barista; he was new, but Dash had the feeling it wouldn't take long for this guy to figure out who Dash and his family were and his order would be remembered, that was usually how things went around Misty Vale, even if Dash did his best to blend in. There just seemed to be something about him that stood out, and people couldn't help but take notice.

He ordered a black coffee, and at the same time, he heard

the door open and close, and he smiled as he saw Amelia walking in. When he saw her again, he felt his dragon stir. He felt the pang of want, the desire to know more, he felt his heart grow with heat, and he had to still himself for a moment, subdue the dragon inside of him and beat it into submission. He had to remain calmer than he felt, when truly, all he wanted to do was grab hold of her and go to town.

She truly was something else. Like no other woman he had seen before, and his dragon knew it. There was something especially intriguing about Amelia. And now, as fate had worked its hand, he was going to be interviewing her for the nanny position to look after Nora.

He just hoped this wasn't going to turn into a terrible idea and conflict of interest.

He smiled and raised his hand, welcoming her as she crossed the room toward him.

"Good morning," she beamed, and he felt her heat and caught her scent. It was turning him on, and he was silent for a moment, his eyes fixed heavy on hers, wondering if she could sense it in him too. She smiled nervously and it broke the spell. He snapped himself back into the here and now and he softened, looking back over his shoulder to the menu that had been written on the chalk board.

"What can I get you?" he asked.

"Oh, I'll take a strong black coffee," she smiled, and Dash couldn't believe his ears.

She was clearly a woman who knew her own mind and had ideas of her own. A black coffee, he really was impressed.

The barista smiled too as if he saw the amusement in them both ordering the same, and then he called to Dash to say that he would bring it over to them.

Dash led the way, and Amelia followed behind him as they went to one of the lower tables with a couch in the alcove. When she sat down, he could see how nervous she was, and he liked it. It made his dragon rage away beneath his skin, and he had to take a moment, again, to compose himself.

What was this woman doing to him?

He cleared his throat and looked deeply into her eyes. He saw her pupils dilate and he bit his lip. She felt it too, he could sense it.

The barista came over and set down the coffees, and Dash and Amelia took a moment, settling themselves and taking a sip, before Amelia clearly worked up the courage to speak first and put herself forward.

"I've brought my resume," Amelia said sweetly as she reached into her handbag and pulled out a folder and slid it across the table to him. "Inside, you'll find references from the last three places I was employed. I included parents as well as agencies. I've been a nanny on and off for around seven years, and before that, I had a wealth of babysitting experience. I've worked in early years settings too at nursery and daycares, and now that I've found myself here in Misty Vale, it would be wonderful to work for a family, getting to know a child on a deeper level, and truly being an influential part of their life."

Dash was impressed. She certainly knew her stuff and had plenty of experience and qualifications. He scanned her resume and then flicked to the references, all of them glowing and with email addresses and telephone numbers so they could be checked. He noticed that most of her experience had been gained on the west coast and it piqued his interest.

"I see you're from California…" he said as he looked up and his eyes caught hers again. "It's a bit of a change coming all the way out here to Misty Vale. What brought you here?"

He could tell she had been expecting the question, but he still felt as if he could sense her heart sinking a little.

"I needed a fresh start," she said as she broke his gaze and looked down at the ground.

Dash looked at the resume again and noticed the gap in her work history. She hadn't been employed for almost the past two years and it instead said she had been babysitting and nannying on an ad hoc basis. He pointed to the section and she breathed in and nodded.

"Over the past two years I've mainly been exploring other avenues," she said. "But I can assure you my knowledge and experience are there, and I am passionate about childcare. Your daughter Nora seems absolutely wonderful, and I feel as if we could genuinely have a great bond if we were to spend some time together."

Dash smiled and nodded.

He could tell that she was holding back on something, that likely in the past two years something had happened to this lady, and for that reason, she had left her hometown and travelled a long way to get to Misty Vale. But he was a good judge of character, and his dragon could sense liars and cheats too, and this woman was not one of them. She had a good heart and soul, and she may have had some adversity, but he could tell she was a genuinely good person who could do with a chance. He looked down at the references again, all of them so lovely and full of praise.

"I think we'll be a good fit," he said with a wry smile, and he was sure he saw a little blush creep across her cheeks. "I'd love it if you could come over for a trial run? I'll check these references today and if you write your number down, I'll give you a call once they've all checked out."

She smiled and nodded enthusiastically and then she scribbled her number on the top of her resume. He watched the way she looped the numbers together and then signed her name. She was so poised and delicate. Man, he wanted to tear her apart in the naughtiest way possible.

When she leaned back and pushed her hair behind her ears, her large blue eyes really stood out to him again and he felt a warm pang in his heart.

"Thank you for meeting with me Dash," she said as she rose to her feet.

"No," he said as he joined her and held out his hand. "Thank you for coming."

She took his hand, and he took it, and the feeling rocketed through them again. She breathed in deeply, her eyes widening, and Dash had to focus on bearing his feet down into the ground to counteract the cosmic shift within him.

This was big.

She was important.

Her hand fell from his and the electricity seemed to linger in the air between them, and as she stepped away from the table and made her way to the door, he knew that he was in trouble.

Dragons don't feel like this for nothing, his inner voice was screaming. This woman is going to change your life.

CHAPTER 5

*D*ash Livingstone. The name had been on the tip of her tongue and rattling around her mind since the second she had met him properly in the lobby of the B&B. He had done nothing but command her thoughts, and now she knew she was gearing up to see him again, she was so nervous she felt as if she could faint.

Dash Livingstone.

What a man.

The second she had lay eyes on him and she had felt something intense between them, she knew she was going to be in trouble. She had come to Misty Vale to find herself, and now she was finding that all she could think about was a man that she barely knew. And not only that, but he was potentially going to be her employer.

She looked at herself in the mirror and noticed the sparkle in her eyes. Since she had broken up with Toby, she had felt so dull and flat, but now she was regaining control and starting again, and she could see that in some ways she was healing. Her eyes seemed alive again, and she couldn't help but wonder whether it had something to do with the new town, or the people she was meeting along the way on her new journey.

He powered his way into her thoughts again.

God, he was sexy.

But he was also slightly terrifying, and Amelia knew that he clearly had the potential to become an overpowering force. She found herself half smiling and half worrying. She was going to have to screw her head back on and stop all of this fantasizing. She was going to be looking after Nora Livingstone and she had to get her head in that instead. It felt good to be finally going back to work properly and to do something that she was passionate about, she couldn't let a man throw her off course. No matter how hot and intimidating he may be.

Dash had called her later on in the afternoon after their meeting at Misty Brews, and he had been happy with her references and that they had all checked out. He said she had clearly made a big impression on a lot of young people's lives, and she was being missed back in her hometown by some of the kids she had babysat across the years. It had been so lovely to hear that, and she was grateful to Dash for telling her. When he had asked if she was still okay to come for a trial run as soon as possible she had been delighted to say yes and now she was ready to step out the door and head over to the Livingstone house. He had given her the address and she had gotten ready quickly. She really didn't want to mess this one up, she needed this job, and for her to be getting so settled and into Misty Vale life after only a day in town was even more amazing.

She grabbed her purse and slipped on her jacket before she headed out into the late evening sun. It was time to show Dash Livingstone what she was all about.

* * *

She could tell that he was a man who dressed well and had fine taste, but she hadn't really thought a whole lot about what Dash's home might look like. When she saw the street that she was pulling into from inside the cab, she knew her mouth was gaping open and she found her hands shaking.

This was more than intimidating.

This was like something she had never seen before in her entire life, and something that she never could have expected.

The houses all along the small, closed off lane, were all ginormous in size and style. They were all different in the way they looked, but the one thing they all had in common was the sheer enormity of them and the flashy cars on the drive. She was supercars, classic cars, some that looked as if they had come from another planet and must have been some of the expensive new electric models that she had heard about in the news. Amelia felt her heart beat faster with nerves, and as the cab pulled up at the bottom of the drive of one of the homes, she was at least a little relieved to see that Dash had a slick black truck parked there and not a bright red sports car.

She stepped out and looked up at the place. It was a huge property that looked as if it had been architecturally designed to the owner's specifications. It looked more traditional than modern, but there was a large pane of glass running down the center showing off the staircase and a dramatic chandelier. It had to be at least three floors high, and she could tell that it must have cost Dash a fortune. For a quiet mountain town, homes like this must have run into the millions and millions of dollars, and she wondered how on earth she had ended up there feeling like a fish out of water.

"Calm down," she coached herself quietly. "You can handle this."

Before she reached the top of the drive and got to the

front door, it was already opening and she could see a very excited Nora jumping up and down, with Dash standing not far behind her. He looked incredible, like he had earlier in the day. But this time he didn't have his long overcoat on, and he had pulled up his sleeves on his sweater. It didn't seem to matter how casual or smart he dressed, he just looked good. He could probably have worn an old sack as a top and still looked incredible. Amelia found herself feeling slightly flustered, but she pushed it down. She wasn't going to let her nerves get the better of her this time. She had waited two long years for this independence and freedom, and she was going to seize it with both hands.

"Hi, Mary Poppins!" Nora said sweetly as Amelia reached the door.

"Well, hello there, Nora," Amelia said in her best British accent before she winked and they both laughed.

Dash smiled and stood back to let Amelia step inside, and when she followed Nora over the threshold, she had to truly stop her mouth from gaping open again when she saw how amazing the house looked. Directly in front of her was a massive staircase that split into two halfway up and wrapped into a gallery balcony all around the first floor. The chandelier that she had been able to see from the street looked even more impressive up closely, and all of its crystals twinkled and glistened above them and reflected on the marble floors underfoot.

"This is quite a house," Amelia said, knowing there was no way she couldn't comment on it without looking foolish or as if she was deliberately avoiding it.

"Daddy designed it," Nora said before Dash had a chance to interject, and he laughed and rubbed his hand down his five-o clock shadow.

"Wow, did you?" Amelia was impressed.

"That's right," he said humbly. "In fact, I had a hand in all of the houses in our little street here. Part of my business is within architecture and planning, so we're pretty well set up for it."

"That all sounds very interesting," Amelia smiled.

"It's boring really," Nora said cheekily. "Even my daddy says so."

Amelia looked up at Dash and they caught each other's eyes and laughed. Nora really was a little spitfire, and Amelia had the feeling she knew exactly where it came from. She was strong and confident, just like her father.

"Well," Dash said. "Why don't we head through to the kitchen and we can show Amelia what you're working on for school tomorrow?" Dash said with a warm smile as he looked down at Nora.

Nora excitedly nodded her head and reached for Amelia's hand, and she led her through the house, past the staircase and into the right-hand side of the property and toward a magnificent kitchen and living area. Amelia was so impressed, the place was huge. And the kitchen was both homely and palatial. Dash had designed a space that incorporated a brilliant cooking space, a place to dine with a long, elegant table, and then at the far end an open plan living area with big L-shaped couches and a huge flat screen on the wall. Behind there was a big set of bi fold doors that gave way to the view of the garden that had been landscaped to perfection. She was sure she could see a pool and a hot tub at the far end on a patio area, a pergola, a wonderful set of outdoor couches that formed another entertaining space with an outdoor kitchen and bar. Behind the garden the pine trees were high and overbearing and they provided complete privacy. It was a stunning home, and Amelia had never imagined anything quite like it.

"Look," Nora said as she led Amelia to the large dining table and let her take in the view of the big pictures and paintings that were scattered around. "We've been learning about the planets," Nora said with a proud smile. "And my teacher asked us to choose and paint our favorite planet, but I like all of them, so I chose three."

Amelia smiled. It may have been mostly large circles filled with dollops of paint, but she could clearly tell what she was looking at and Nora definitely had a talent.

"Well, isn't this amazing," Amelia grinned. "I can see that we have Earth, Mars, and is that one Saturn?" she pointed to the rings that looped around the last planet perfectly.

"Yes," Nora smiled. "I like Earth the best because it's where we live."

Dash and Amelia caught each other's eyes and he smiled and raised his eyebrows.

"Can I get you something to drink?" he asked.

Amelia nodded.

"I have coffee, sparkling water, soda?"

"Sparkling water would be fantastic," Amelia replied, and she watched as he moved over to the large refrigerator and opened one of the doors. Inside it appeared to be all drinks, and it wasn't long before she clocked on that in fact, he had four refrigerator doors lining the wall.

"This is the drinks," he said, as if reading her mind. "Then this door is food, the next freezer and the last, well that's kind of just anything." He laughed.

He placed a glass down in front of Amelia and began to pour. Just feeling him over her shoulder made her heart pound and her stomach knot into a tight squeeze of excitement. He was so hot, and so controlled, and it made her want to throw all of her control out the window and pounce on him. She didn't know where it was coming from, this intense desire, but it was so strong and felt so right that it was unnerving her.

You can't feel this way, she told herself internally. You just can't.

She knew she had moved away from her hometown to start again as an independent woman on her own, and she really didn't want to get into a relationship again where she felt like she was losing herself. She had to remain strong and fight these feelings. She was working for the man for God's sake.

Dash sat down opposite her, and they caught each other's eye again. Between them Nora was chattering away about the solar system and drawing big colorful circles in the correct order to show them exactly what was there and how it was laid out. But Dash and Amelia were focused fully on each other, she could sense it. She saw the way his eyes flicked over hers, the way he breathed and the way he was watching her. She couldn't tell whether it was because he was sizing her up to see if she was good enough to be in charge of his daughter and spend so much time in his home, or whether he was as intrigued by her as she was by him.

The night passed by in a lovely way, with the three of them eating dinner together, Dash showed Amelia where everything was in the kitchen, and they laughed and joked together as they cooked pizza from scratch and let Nora pick the toppings. After a couple of hours in the Livingstone house, Amelia felt right at home, and it was clear that she and Nora had bonded fast, just as she had expected. When it came time for Nora to go to bed, Amelia said goodbye to them both at the door as her cab pulled up the driveway. It had been such a wonderful night she didn't want to leave.

"So," Dash said as he looked down at his daughter and patted her on the shoulder. "Did you enjoy having Amelia here with us tonight?"

"I loved it, Daddy!" Nora beamed. "She is so much fun and so much better than the other nanny's you've had here. Please can she stay, please can she?"

Amelia smiled and Dash cocked his head to the side.

"Well I guess that's up to Amelia, if she feels that this is something she would like to make a regular thing… A proper thing?"

They had already discussed what the routine would be when it came to Nora's care, and it sounded like the perfect set up. It was almost too good to be true.

"I would love to," Amelia smiled, not wanting to let Nora wait a second longer for her answer. "I would love to nanny for you Nora, I think you and I will have great fun together."

"Yay!" Nora said excitedly as she clapped her hands together and jumped up and down on the spot. "I have my own real-life Mary Poppins!"

Dash and Amelia laughed, and they looked into each other's eyes.

"Well," Amelia said as she took a step back away from the house. "I had a great time tonight, and I'll be seeing you both…?"

"How about we start the day after tomorrow?" he asked. "That way you can at least unpack your bags here in town before throwing yourself straight into work."

His eyes glistened and it made her feel warm all over.

"Perfect," she smiled.

She waved goodbye as she climbed into the cab, and couldn't believe it when she saw the time and it was almost 10pm. Nora had stayed up so late, but it was clear that it had been needed for them all tonight. She imagined she was an early riser anyway and could no doubt have a little bit of a lie in before school in the morning.

As the cab made its way back to the B&B, Amelia was on cloud nine, but she also had her reservations. Her and Dash were now being thrown together properly, and whatever she was feeling for him she was going to have to bury deep. She was working for him now… and she wanted to do her very best.

She may have felt pulled to him on a more intimate level… but it was time to toe the line and have some self-control.

"You don't even know if he even likes you…" she whispered almost silently to herself.

But that wasn't technically true… she felt it.

She felt it more than she had ever felt anything.

CHAPTER 6

*D*ash stepped out of his truck and tossed the keys to the valet. The kid was new, but he could tell that he already was fully aware who Dash was and he stumbled as he went to catch them and then was overly apologetic.

"It's okay," Dash said with a warm smile. "Don't worry about it."

The Golf Club was a place he and his family had been coming since the moment it had opened, hell, they did own the place. And whenever he set foot here, he appreciated how attentive and polite the staff were to him, but sometimes he also just wished for a little anonymity. He wasn't the type of guy who looked for special treatment, but it seemed to come with the territory of being a Livingstone.

He stepped inside the big, gilded doors to a flurry of hello's and good mornings as he made his way along to the club room. He had a meeting there with his family and brothers in arms in less than an hour, but before he jumped headfirst into business, he wanted to unpack the past few days.

It had been a total whirlwind, and his head was as fucked

up as it had ever been.

Amelia.

The new nanny he had hired for Nora, was keeping him awake at night. He took a seat at a table overlooking the green and ordered a black coffee and a shot of bourbon. He wanted to keep the fire inside him burning and also take the edge of what had been a day filled with uncertainly and second guessing himself.

He felt the change in him, and it was making him nervous.

He had heard his kind talk about what it was like to find their one true mate... but he had always assumed it would never happen to him. Not after what had gone down with Nora's mother and the way she had left them the way she did. Since then he had always vowed never to fall in love, and to never even consider finding another mate. Never mind the one true person he was supposed to be with.

He had been used for his money, taken for granted for the lifestyle he could give to women, and then left in the dust with a baby in his arms and no idea of what he was doing. It had been the darkest moment of his life, but luckily, Nora had been a shining light for him.

The only thing that had pulled him through.

He breathed in deeply and sighed.

How could he unpack and dismantle all the things he was feeling? How could he even begin to try and understand them? They were so intense and all so new, and it was frightening in a good way, but it also made him want to run.

He was a dragon shifter... a powerful force. And the fact that he was so drawn to this woman, that he lusted after her, longed for her, and craved her in such an intense way, made him afraid not just for himself, but for her too.

She was working for him now, and he didn't want to be in a relationship. He didn't want her to see all the trappings that came with having the wealth he did, the fact that he could never truly trust after what he had been through. He could feel in his bones that Amelia was different, she had an innocent and genuine soul. But he still had his reservations, and the fact that she was working for him made it all the more difficult. Even though it was also wonderful because he got to see her on a daily basis.

He thought of her coming into his life. How he had almost knocked her down outside the B&B, and the way the fire inside him had ignited when he looked into her eyes. He had known then, in an instant, that she was going to be someone very important to him, and he had spent the rest of that day and night obsessing over her. Thinking about her, of who she was, of what she was doing in his little mountain town, and when he had gone back to the B&B the next day to check on business, he would be lying if he said he hadn't been hoping to see her.

And then he *had* seen her... and Maude had almost matchmaker-ed them on a professional level and suggested that Amelia could be a good fit as Nora's nanny.

And wow, was she a good fit.

He had never seen his daughter take so well to another woman. She had loved her from the moment she had seen her, and the two of them had got along famously all night when Amelia had come for a trial run at the house. They had even completely lost track of time.

But now he was conflicted.

He had Nora to think about, not himself. And even though his dragon was stirring more than ever, and that his instincts had kicked into overdrive to want to protect Amelia, he had to be realistic.

"You can't pursue this," he said to himself. "She's working for you, and you can't give into your urges."

The server arrived with his coffee and his shot of bourbon. He thanked him and then knocked the shot back before he sighed and felt the warmth spread through him. It was just what he needed.

He looked out across the green and saw the golfers with their carts and caddy's moving in the distance. He had a lot to be proud of, he and his family had done amazing things in this town. Sometimes, it was hard to process it all.

When he saw Striker and some of his other brothers and pack members start to file into the club room, he shook out his shoulders and breathed in deep. They had a lot to discuss. Not least the fact that bikers had apparently been sniffing around because of the up and coming Oktoberfest, but also, the long-standing feud they had with a rival pack in town. The goddam bears. It may have been peaceful for many years now, but the tension always lingered, and of late, something seemed to have change.

He felt, and all the dragons could sense, that there was an animosity growing, and it was time they discussed and assessed it properly. The town of Misty Vale may have appeared perfect, but there was a lot of deep secrets buried there, and a lot of tension flowing below the surface.

He thought back to the rumors of The Grand Lodge, of what had apparently started it all, and it made his blood chill. So many secrets and lies... so many decades of bad feelings running between two families that had echoed out into the community. And now he and his brothers of the here and now were likely going to have to try and uncover it all, while also making sure the town didn't erupt into a shit storm.

The last thing he had time for was his fated mate turning up.

What was he thinking getting all carried away with his longings? Dash Livingstone was going to have to lock his dragon away and try to fight what he knew was fate.

Even if it destroyed him in the process.

CHAPTER 7

$\mathcal{A}$melia wandered along Main Street with a smile on her face and a feeling of hope in her heart. She was on her way to see Jane, the beautician, after a wonderful day in Misty Vale, settling herself into town life even more and really getting to know the place.

She had gone into some of the stores along Main Street and had met some of the workers and owners, she had also found out a few interesting rumors about The Grand Lodge that was perched high up on the mountainside and looked down over them all. It had certainly been an interesting day to hear about the legends that clung to the place, about the fact that some of the residents believed there was treasure buried there, and that some of the older buildings, the lodge included, were haunted. She had even discovered that there were ghost tours in operation around town for the tourists and it was one of Misty Vale's most well-loved attractions, along with a proper tourist center where they organized horseback ridings and hikes to some of the more scenic locations. With it coming into fall, it certainly looked like the ghost tours were going to be popular, especially with the upcoming Oktoberfest guaranteed to bring in a lot of tourists, and Amelia had realized that she had come to town at a particularly exciting time. Misty Vale was a buzzing hive of activity, and it was awesome to feel included and to have so much going on around her. When she thought back to the life she had been living only a week before, one that felt so stale and boring, one that wasn't fulfilling her in anyway, she couldn't believe that she had turned her life around so fast and was now looking forward to getting up in the mornings. It was awesome and she was loving every second.

As she opened the door to Jane's and stepped inside, she felt the warmth hit her and she couldn't help but smile again. It had been such a long time since she had given herself any true thought or had been able to just make her own decisions when it came to the way she looked and how she wanted to present herself. She had always been told to do the right thing, to do as a man wanted, but this time it was all down to her. And she couldn't wait to get started.

"Hey there girl," Jane buzzed as Amelia closed the door behind her and started to slip her jacket off from around her shoulders. "How are you doing?"

"I'm really well," Amelia smiled. "How are you? Have you had another busy day?"

"Oh, it's been hectic but I'm all good," Jane grinned. "I'm just glad that business is booming, I can never complain."

"Totally," Amelia said as she crossed the room and Jane took her jacket from her and showed her to a table set in front of a mirror.

"What can I get you to drink?" Jane said. "Some places around here are a little tight when it comes to looking after their customers but I'm the total opposite, plus I have a nice bottle of wine chilling out back if you feel like unwinding?"

"That sounds fantastic," Amelia laughed. Her time in Misty Vale really did keep getting better and better.

Jane brought her a nice cool glass of white wine, and she took a sip. She hadn't been on a night out or anywhere near a bar in over a year, so this felt like she was truly letting her hair down and allowing herself to indulge.

Jane smiled at her in the mirror and started to run her hands through Amelia's hair, taking her fingertips all the way down to the bottom and scrutinizing the ends.

"I know," Amelia said with embarrassment. "It's terrible."

"You can say that again," Jane said playfully. "They've split more time than I can count. When was the last time you visited a hairdresser?"

"I really can't remember," Amelia admitted. "It's been far too long though, and I'm looking forward to making it right."

"Well, we can certainly do that, and you've come to the right place This is your night to pamper yourself senseless. Hair first, then nails and brows… what do you think?"

"That sounds amazing," Amelia said as she sighed down into the chair and took another sip of wine.

"So, did you have a think about what you wanted to do?" Jane asked as she pulled up a seat and grabbed a color chart from on the side. She passed it to Amelia and let her attention be drawn to the amazing different shades of browns, blonds, reds, and even some more daring purples and blues.

"I think I want to go a little lighter and richer," she smiled. "I haven't touched my hair in so long, I may as well freshen it up."

"Sounds good to me!" Jane said as she leaned forward and pointed to a honey blonde. "What do you think of this? It'll mean we don't need to use bleach, but it'll warm your color up and keep the fairness?"

"Perfect," Amelia grinned.

She relaxed back onto the chair and watched as Jane mixed the colors and started to apply them to her hair slowly. This was the perfect end to such a fabulous day, and she truly felt that in Jane she could make a friend.

A couple of hours later, and Amelia was reborn. After her hair had been colored and they were waiting for it to take, Jane had led her over to the nail bar where Amelia had picked out a rich plum shade and had her nails manicured and nourished. After the color had been taken out of her hair and she had it cut so the ends were blunt and new, she watched as Jane dried it with a big roller brush and gave it lots of volume and bounce. When she saw herself in the mirror, she almost couldn't believe how much better she looked. It was as if she faded out version of herself was long gone, and the old Amelia was finally staring back at her, with her eyes dazzling bright.

"How come you left it so long?" Jane asked over the noise of the dryer as she finished the last few wet strands of hair.

"If I'm honest I was in kind of a terrible relationship," Amelia admitted. "I felt as if he controlled me and I lost all sense of who I was. And some issues I had with my mom only played into that too… she always told me I was the problem, that I had to make my man happy and wear the right clothes, have the right make-up and always make sure my hair was perfect. It all kind of sent me the other way. I tried for so long to keep up with all those expectations, but in the end, I didn't know who I was anymore. I looked in the mirror and I saw a girl who was overdone, and I didn't like it. I just wanted to be me… plain and simple. I didn't want to have to wake up in the morning, jump straight in the shower and put on a full face of make-up and make sure my hair was immaculate. I wanted to just scrape back my hair somedays and worry about that later, if at all."

"Wow," Jane said sadly. "That really sucks. I can't believe your mom told you to do all that stuff."

"I know now it was wrong," Amelia said. "But at the time I

just thought I was the one who was crazy. Like why couldn't I just be perfect and then my relationship would be too? But as time went on and I saw how he was and who he was becoming too, I knew it didn't matter what I wore or how I looked, he was still going to walk all over me and I wasn't going to get myself back."

"So, you left?" Jane asked.

Amelia nodded.

"I broke up with him and then I planned my escape from that place, it was time to start again. And when I found myself here, I didn't know what to expect, but I just knew I wanted to find the old Amelia. To bring her back and to feel like myself again, and being here tonight with you and doing this, is really helping."

Jane rested her hand on Amelia's shoulder and gave her a warm smile in the mirror, it was full of sympathy and understanding.

"I've been with controlling men too," Jane said. "And I know how tough it can be... So, I have to tell you that I think you're incredibly brave and strong. You are doing amazing."

"Thank you," Amelia said. "And thank you for this, for staying open so late for me and doing all of this. I feel incredible."

"And we still have eyebrows to go!" Jane laughed as she shut off the hairdryer. "I'm all done with your hair, so why don't you jump over onto that seat on the other side of the room and we can thread them for you before we finish?"

"Yes ma'am," Amelia said as she rose to her feet and ran her hands through her fresh hair. It really did look amazing, and she saw the girl she used to be starting back at her. The girl from long before Toby, before she listened too much to her mom's own insecurities, and the girl who had been focused on her career and her future.

She would be her again, and as she sat down in the next

chair ready for the final part of her pamper and makeover, Amelia knew that she was feeling better than she had done in some years.

"You know," Jane said as she tipped the chair back and started to study Amelia's eyebrows. "You're new in town, we should hit the bars one night so I can show you what this place is all about!"

"I would love that," Amelia grinned. "I can't remember the last time I had a night out."

"Well, it's always fun around here," Jane laughed. "Any night of the week."

"I start my new job tomorrow so I may be a little busy for a week or so, but I would love to the moment I get some time off."

"A new job already, wow, you really are smashing it here in Misty Vale!" Jane beamed. "Where are you going to be working?"

"I'm actually going to be a nanny for a little girl," she said warmly. "I'm so looking forward to it, she's an absolute dream."

"So cute," Jane smiled. "And who are her mom and dad? I might know them, you tend to find that most of the women come through here at some point."

"Well, actually…" Amelia faltered, not knowing what to say, because she wasn't sure what had happened to Nora's mom. "I don't know the mother… but the father is called Dash Livingstone."

It seemed the only way she could put it. It was clear that Dash was single, but for all she knew, the mom could still be around somewhere.

She noticed the look on Jane's face, it must have been similar to the dropped jaw look Amelia had been rocking when she walked into the Livingstone house the night before.

"Dash Livingstone?" Jane asked, her eyes wild with excitement. "Wow... I mean, *wow.*"

Amelia smiled but again, didn't quite know what to say. She didn't want to say anything, considering he was her new boss. And she had the feeling about him too... the one she couldn't shake.

"You know him then?" Amelia asked.

"Oh yes," Jane smiled. "I know him all right. Everyone in town does. He's from a very powerful family. One of the original families that founded Misty Vale in fact."

This made Amelia even more nervous, but she kept her cool, trying not to act too interested. A founding family... it sounded like he had quite the reputation and a large dynasty. If everyone in town knew Dash, then it seemed even more crazy that he had found Amelia and plucked her from obscurity to be Nora's nanny. But he had told her Nora hadn't bonded with anyone he had interviewed, and she had to give herself credit where it was due, Amelia did have good experience and references.

"All I can say is, once you're in with the Livingstone's, you're in with Misty Vale royalty," Jane continued. "You couldn't have fallen more on your feet with a job. Let me tell you."

Misty Vale royalty.

Now her head truly was spinning.

Dash Livingstone was becoming more and more of an enigma by the second. And Amelia was determined to crack his code.

ash had watched how well Amelia and Nora were bonding every day when he returned from work and they were sat together on the couch in the living area of the kitchen. He usually found them reading Nora's book that had been sent home by her teachers, or doing some math or art, occasionally they would be playing with toys if the work sent home had been completed and Amelia had already been looking into classes for Nora to begin in town. It was crazy how easily into a routine they seemed to have got in a short space of time. It had only been a few days, but already the girls had established a real connection, and it was clear they were settled into their new life with each other. It was working well, with Dash doing the morning routine as normal and getting Nora to school, Amelia would usually get the groceries on her way to collect her on the afternoon, take her anywhere she needed to go and then get her home for dinner and homework, a bath and sorted before Dash came home. The past couple of days, she had also started to make sure there was something waiting for Dash to eat too, and he couldn't have been more grateful. It had been a long time since he had felt looked after by anyone, let alone a beautiful woman.

It was doing things to his head, and his resolve that he had been so determined to keep was already starting to slip.

Amelia was an incredible woman, and he felt lucky to have found her at just the right time.

"She loves the idea of dancing," Amelia had grinned when her and Dash were sitting up at the counter as dinner was cooking on the stove. "I mean, I know all little girls do, but she has mentioned it several times now."

Dash didn't want to deny Nora anything, and to hear all of these inner desires coming through Amelia was fascinating. He knew that she wanted to explore other things way from the golf club and the kids' activities they had there, but to hear she wanted to focus on dance specifically was lovely to know.

"I'm happy for her to explore any avenue," Dash said as he smiled at Amelia. "I can tell how much she is growing up with each passing day and it's one of the reasons I didn't want to be dragging her to business meetings after school all the time. She needs to be exploring her passions and finding out who she truly is."

Amelia had seemed to swoon a little when he said that. He had noticed immediately the blush spread across her chest and the way she had reached up and touched her neck.

The truth was he was finding it harder and harder to keep his distance from her. She was a breath of fresh air when it came to the people he knew around Misty Vale, she kept it simple and didn't complicate anything. She was her own person, she didn't seem phased by his house or by who he was, and she certainly didn't flirt or seem to want to throw herself at him. He was used to women using their good looks and their power to try and entice him, whereas Amelia was just a genuinely good soul. Someone who was looking after him and his daughter, while also being incredibly level-headed. It was sending his inner dragon into a frenzy.

"She's such a great kid," Amelia smiled. "I feel very blessed to be working with her."

"I think we're the blessed ones," Dash told her honestly. "You really are like a Mary Poppins, all jokes aside. You've brought out a lovely side in my daughter and I can see how happy she is. I was worried she was getting down before we hired you, but you've brought her back to her best self."

Amelia smiled shyly and looked at the floor. Every time he caught her eye or paid her a compliment, she seemed to shy away from it as if he made her nervous. And he couldn't help but be turned on by that, it was so endearing.

"Well, I better get going," Amelia said as she grabbed her purse from the counter and stepped back toward Nora who was sitting and reading her books in the living area. She looked so engrossed, Dash knew that Amelia was reluctant to break the spell, but it was getting late and it was time for bed.

"Can't you stay a little longer?" Nora asked with wide eyes.

"Well, I would love to honey, but it's your bedtime and you need to spend some quality time with your dad."

Dash smiled, she really was very sweet.

Stay down Dragon, he told himself.

"Aww," Nora pouted. "I'll miss you Amelia…"

Amelia bent down and gave the little girl a hug. Dash watched as she wrapped her arms around Amelia's neck and breathed her in deep. It stirred something in him, and it made him feel a pang of something he hadn't felt in a long time. A longing for a true family unit, the fact that he needed the stability as much as Nora did.

He didn't know how to stop himself from falling in deep… but he knew he had to try. He had to keep himself strong. He didn't want to ruin this.

. . .

AS HE WATCHED THE CAB PULL AWAY AND HE WAITED BY THE door, he knew something was changing within him. He felt the intense fire burning hard and the need for release. It had been at least a week since he had shifted, but once he got Nora to bed and fast asleep, he headed outside into the garden and looked up at the moon.

When he and his company had built the houses on their quiet little street, they had factored in privacy as a major issue. The other huge homes were occupied by other dragons, other members of his pack and his brotherhood who also loved the quiet nature of where they were and the fact that they had complete privacy and direct access to the large pine forest.

Dash secured the property before he left, and once he was in the garden, he let the dragon take hold of him. He felt his whole frame shudder and his skin split open to reveal the intense scales. He felt his limbs elongating, the fire on the tip of his tongue and the intense power he possessed. He would have to be fast, but he was on high alert and he knew that Nora was safe, she was in her bed fast asleep and he was just outside. If anything were to change, his instinct would tell him immediately, he just had to get his fix, he had to let his body become the inner beast, to transform into the almighty dragon that held his heart.

When he was standing tall and proud as the dragon he could see above the rooftop of his home, he could see Nora through the window sleeping soundly in her bed and he felt the rush of energy burst through him as he pushed off from the ground and powered into the sky. He looked down at his home, sitting there safely and at the rest of Misty Vale. The twinkling lights were so stunning, and his town was perfect. He truly did love it there. His eyes flickered to The Grand

Lodge and he felt a shudder of apprehension. He knew trouble was coming, he could sense it, and he felt as if it could have something to do with that place. With the legends that had circulated for years, and the ancient ruins that were still there behind the main structure of the hotel that had been rebuilt, there was something sinister about it in a lot of ways. But he was still drawn to it, as were most of the people of Misty Vale. He could have stayed up there forever, looking across the land, but he quickly brought himself back down. He and his kind had to be careful, when they shifted, they usually went up into the mountains, but sometimes, the feeling took over and that was why they had their big, private and secluded homes.

When Dash touched down, he looked through the window again to see Nora sleeping soundly, and then he began the process of turning back into his human form. As he shrunk back down and his scales gave way to skin, he called out at the moon as the heat and fire subsided.

He was so conflicted and yet becoming the dragon had given him the answers he needed. He had to stop resisting how he felt about Amelia. There was something there between them, something that was impossible to deny. He knew she felt it too, and the way he had latched onto her, the way his heart had called out for her, after just one glance was the biggest tell of all.

She was his fated mate. The one he had never thought would arrive. The one he had thought would be myth or legend. After Nora's mother had left them and broken both he and Nora's hearts, he had never thought something like this could happen for him. He assumed he would be destined to walk the earth alone… but now Amelia had come to Misty Vale, and it was fate.

He had to have her. He had to protect her at all costs and make sure she was safe. He didn't know what was happening around town for sure, but with the tension rising in the air, he had the feeling he and his pack were going to have their work cut out for them.

And he wondered how Amelia would respond if she ever found out what he truly was. Would she run from him? Or would she embrace it?

She sighed and looked up at the moon, his clothes in torn and tattered shreds on the ground around him. He was standing there naked and asking the heavens for answers he knew they couldn't give.

He had never felt this laid bare or this vulnerable, and yet he had never felt so strong either. Amelia had awoken something in him, something important and powerful, and now he was going to embrace it all and move forwards.

A dragon can't deny his fate…

His father had told him that when he was a child and was coming into his own power, and only now did he truly know what that meant.

Amelia was his fate.

And it was time for Dash to succumb to the powers at be.

CHAPTER 9

Amelia looked in the mirror and smiled as she checked out her new boots and the lovely faux leather jacket and fur trim she was about to buy. She had headed out early in the day to hit the shops of Misty Vale properly, and she had spent a lot of time choosing these particular pieces. She hadn't been shopping for herself in over a year, and it felt wonderful to be picking some things for her wardrobe that she knew she could wear time and time again. With the cooler weather coming in fast, it was good to know she had some staple items to take her all the way through autumn and winter.

So far, she had been in the bookstore and bought a new romance novel, something she had always loved to indulge in before she met Toby, and she had also visited a few of the boutiques and gift stores. It appeared Misty Vale was indeed gearing up for a very busy few weeks with the Oktoberfest coming to town and the influx of tourists it would no doubt bring. With the leaves also starting to turn, she heard from one of the store owners that they were used to seeing a lot of photographers at this time of year. Influencers and more traditional photographers who worked for magazines came to Misty Vale in droves to take pictures of their wonderful landscape and then publicized it all to the world.

When she had paid for her new items, Amelia headed down the street toward one of the smaller restaurants and went inside. She was absolutely starving and when she saw how delightful it was in there, she was glad she had picked this particular place. It had low lighting and a lovely fire burning away in one corner of the room. The tables were all mismatched and so were the chairs, and the artwork on the walls was quirky and old fashioned. She was shown to a table in the window and she sat down and opened the menu, looking at what delights she could sample from yet another one of Misty Vale's wonderful independent businesses.

She had barely been sitting for five minutes when she felt a tingle roll over her hands and up her arm and she felt compelled to look outside. It was the strangest feeling, as if something deep inside of her had come alive and was urging her to follow their lead. When she saw what she was looking at, she became even more stunned, as she was looking at Dash moving slowly across the street with a file under his arm as if he had just come from a meeting. Her heart skipped a beat, and she bit her lip. He looked amazing as always, dressed in a long black overcoat, cashmere sweater and a pair of black jeans. She felt her skin tingle again, and then to her complete surprise it was as if she had just called out his name or something, he stopped still right outside the window and his eyes flicked up directly to hers.

She was staring at him with wide eyes, and he back at her, but before long his face broke into a smile and he held up his hand and waved. He had come from right across the street and out of nowhere, but it was as if he had known she was there on instinct, the moment he was close enough, and when their eyes met she felt a pang of want deep in her heart.

She waved back and smiled, even though they must have only been a few feet away and separated by a pane of glass. He looked down at his watch and then back at her and then he cocked his head to the side. He could see that she was still looking at the menu and that she didn't even have a drink in front of her, and within an instant, she almost felt as if she heard his mind make the decision before he moved.

He was going to come in and join her. She just knew it.

She watched as he laughed and moved toward the doorway of the restaurant and when he came inside, he spoke to the waitress and pointed over to the table where Amelia was sitting.

When he came over, she rose to her feet and he smiled.

"Fancy some company?" he asked. "I mean, if you don't mind me gatecrashing your quiet and peaceful lunch."

"That would be lovely," she said as they both sat back down, and Dash put the folder out of sight and under the table out of the way.

"Well, this is a coincidence," Amelia said. "But it's great to see a friendly face."

Dash smiled, as if he knew a secret. And then he nodded slowly.

"It's good to see you Amelia, and out of a working environment this time. Even if it doesn't feel like work when you're at home with us, but you know what I mean."

"I do," she said.

"How's your day going so far," his eyes met hers and she saw something in them that she had never seen in another person's before. Something fiery and fierce.

"It's going well thank you," she said, trying not to let herself get distracted. "I thought I would explore town some more and check out some of these wonderful stores that are scattered around the place. Back where I'm from, it's a lot of chains and large corporations. But I love it here because it's the opposite."

"Me too," Dash beamed. "It certainly makes it feel special doesn't it?"

The waitress approached the table and Dash ordered a glass of red wine.

"Will you join me?" he asked.

"Sure," Amelia smiled. "Why not. Also, I'm open to recommendations on food…"

Dash smiled at her and flicked out his menu. He scanned it and then his eyes travelled up to hers again.

"It has to be the spaghetti marinara, simple and classic, but from here it is oh so good. And it goes well with the wine too," he clipped the menu closed and passed his back to the waitress.

"Okay," Amelia smiled. "That sounds amazing to me."

Dash ordered two of the spaghetti dishes and within a few moments the waitress was back at the table with a very old-looking bottle of wine. Amelia watched as she uncorked it and poured a small amount into the glass in front of Dash. He took hold of the glass by the stem and brought it to his face, sniffing the wine before tasting it longingly. He looked up at the waitress and nodded and then she began to pour more for him and a glass for Amelia.

"You clearly know your stuff," Amelia said once the waitress had walked away.

"To be honest, I don't have a clue," Dash laughed. "I just know how to make the right noise when faced with situations like this, it comes from years of being taken to fancy restaurants by my parents."

Amelia laughed.

"For all I know we could be drinking a cheap bottle from the liquor store."

He shrugged and then leaned back in his chair. He looked

so relaxed, more so that Amelia had ever seen him. And having him close to her again, in this kind of chilled environment was making her want things she didn't dare admit.

"So, how are you finding things looking after Nora?" he asked. "I won't make it all about work don't worry," he half smiled. "I'm just hoping you're settling in all right."

"I'm settling in more than all right," Amelia smiled. "I love your daughter, she's fantastic. We get along so well, and I truly hope we can continue to success in bonding."

Dash's eyes seemed to come alive when she said the words and she felt herself nervously reach for the wine, she twisted the glass by the stem and breathed in deep.

"I feel as if I want to ask you though..." she knew she had to tread carefully. "What happened to Nora's mom? Is she still in the picture? I mean, purely from a work perspective... I was just wondering if she was in town or whether I may have to take her further afield some days."

"It's okay," Dash looked almost relieved. "I'm glad you asked."

She knew he could tell that she hadn't just asked for work reasons, that she was clearly wondering because of him too, but he didn't say anything. He just leaned in a little closer and began.

"We were together for maybe a year before Nora was born," he said. "It all happened quite quickly... and I don't think she ever truly loved me. Once Nora was born, she seemed to just want to be back out on the party scene. There isn't a big one here in Misty Vale, so she would go out to other towns with her friends, stay out until dawn and leave me with the baby. She was never truly cut out to be a mother, and it only took a matter of months after Nora was born and she had packed her bags and left. She said she didn't want to be tied down. The last I heard she was partying her way across Europe and has found herself some wealthy man to marry. I guess everyone is different." He raised his eyebrows and then he took a sip of his wine.

His face was calm, and he didn't look upset or bothered, but Amelia couldn't help but let her jaw sag open and the shock ooze out of her.

"My God," she whispered. "That is not what I was expecting."

"I didn't expect it either," Dash half laughed. "But I should have known from the start, the warning signs were always there. She was far too impressed by material possessions. Far too bothered about having the best of the best rather than just enjoying life. I think I was targeted and used… when she realized I wanted to settle and live a humbler life as a little family with our baby… she just wasn't interested."

"But… Nora…" Amelia said with disbelief. "How could she just walk away?"

"Well, I'll never understand that either," Dash admitted. "But we are better off without her."

It was a brutal statement, but one Amelia could already tell to be true. No child should be rejected like that. It was just so harsh.

"I'm sorry," Amelia said genuinely. "It must have been very hard going through that."

"It was," Dash nodded, his eyes settling on hers. "But we have come out stronger, and I know now what I want and what I don't want."

His eyes seemed to burn into hers and it made her heart race. She felt as if the words were solely directed at her, as if he wanted her to listen to them and take them in.

He knows what he wants and what he doesn't want.

And so do I.

She smiled and she had the urge to reach for his hand, but she resisted, until he did it first. His palm closed over the top of hers and almost stopped her heart. She felt the intense heat coming from him, a power that she didn't understand but something she was beginning to crave. Their energies seemed to be fusing together and as she looked into his eyes, she saw fire. It made her gasp, but she wasn't afraid. She wanted to feel it, she wanted to experience him and know what he was all about.

"Dash," she whispered. "I know there's something different about you."

He didn't speak, but his expression told her all she needed to know.

"I feel it… I want to know…"

He smiled.

"You will know," he told her. "I want you to be with us…"

It made her spine tingle and she quivered. It was the single most romantic thing anyone had ever said to her.

He wanted her to be with them.

"There is something very, very special about you Amelia," Dash said. "And I'm finding it very hard to stop myself from being close to you."

She swallowed nervously. The thought of him being even closer to her right now made her whole body come alive, it made her heart race, and her bones shake. All she could think about was jumping across the table and ripping his clothes off… but she had to be strong. This man was doing very strange things to her. Things she hadn't expected.

"I felt something…" she decided to be brave and tell him. "The moment I first saw you… it was so strange, as if you were watching me after you had walked away. I felt it all the time, as if you were there, kind of like a part of me had changed."

Dash's hand gave hers a reassuring squeeze.

"I don't know how else to explain it…" she said. "But all I know is that I can't believe I'm being so open with you, and this whole thing scares me to death. I don't want to compromise anything."

"You're not," he said. "What you felt is completely normal. For what I am…" he stopped himself and pulled his hand away. It took her by surprise, and once his heat had left her directly, she felt like she was aching for it again.

"What you are?" she asked.

Before Dash had chance to answer, the waitress was back at the table with their meals and she set them down and broke the flow of the conversation. Amelia couldn't believe all that was happening here, but something deeply had changed between them now. They had opened their hearts to each other, and it was clear their feelings were being reciprocated.

After they were alone at the table again, they dove into more relaxed conversation, but they kept catching each other's eyes and Amelia knew they would go back to it again and he would be honest and open with her.

They talked about their lives before they had met, and Amelia even opened up to him about her past relationship. Dash admitted her guessed it must have been a guy that had sent her seeking a new life and he was impressed that she had the nerve to start again somewhere entirely new.

"Why don't we go and collect Nora together?" Dash said once they had finished and were standing outside on the street. "I can take the rest of the day off, we can get her settled at home and finish up our conversation properly."

Amelia smiled and agreed. She couldn't have hoped for a better end to the most unexpectedly awesome day.

She was going back to the Livingstone home once again, and this time, she hoped she was going to get some answers.

CHAPTER 10

*O*nce homework was done, dinner had been cooked and eaten, and Nora was safely tucked up in bed, Dash and Amelia sunk down into the comfy couches in the living area and Dash opened another bottle of wine. They had had the most perfect day together, and it was a shame to bring it to an end.

"Now this one," Dash said as he held up the wine bottle started to pour into the two long stemmed wine glasses. "Is one I do know… and it's a good one. My family sell it up at the golf resort."

"A golf resort too huh?" Amelia asked with a little laugh. "You really do own most of the town."

"Not most…" Dash winked. "But yes, quite a bit. I guess it comes with the territory of being one of the founding families here."

"Tell me about Misty Vale," she smiled. "I'm intrigued to learn more about this place, it seems to have a very interesting history."

Dash took a sip and leaned back into the couch, wrapping his arm around Amelia's shoulder as they both looked into the dancing flames of the fire he had lit earlier in the night. The logs were crackling and snapping in the fire, making the whole room glow with red.

"Oh, it is full of mystery and secrets," he said ominously but Amelia could tell that he was teasing. "And I guess it all begins with The Grand Lodge. Have you seen it?"

Amelia nodded.

"The huge hotel on the mountain, right?" she asked.

"That's the one," Dash continued. "Well, way back when the first settlers came here, my ancestors included, there were a couple of families that were always fighting over things. Land, trade, power in general… and it all kind of culminated in some kind of feud surrounding the lodge. It was built originally when the first people founded Misty Vale, but something happened afterwards… the details are all kind of sketchy, but basically the original lodge was destroyed and a new one was built in its place round about the twenties and the prohibition era. Since then there's been all sorts of legends about it being haunted, of supernatural beasts and creatures living in secret around these parts. And one of my personal favorites, that somewhere under the ruins of the original lodge, there is a treasure buried."

He paused and looked at Amelia who was watching him wide eyed. He wasn't sure how she was going to react, but she seemed completely enthralled.

"What kind of supernatural creatures?" she asked sitting up slightly. She was rapt in the story.

"A vampire, a fairy… men who can turn into animals and beasts…" he said it delicately, almost expecting her to laugh, but she didn't.

"I love stuff like that," she said with a beaming smile. "And I always knew that somewhere out of the main cities, there would be little towns with their legends, and I think it's awesome. I hope it is true."

She grinned and looked into the fire.

"I mean why not?" she said. "People see ghosts all the time… if this town has been here for well over a hundred years, then of course there are going to be some spirits lurking around. I believe in it all because I am certain I've seen a ghost before in my past. And I mean one hundred percent sure."

She paused and looked up at him and he felt his heart swell. She really was a kind and innocent soul. Most of the women he had met in the past would have snorted and laughed at him for telling her the history of Misty Vale and past it off as rubbish, they wouldn't have entertained for a moment that it could be in any way true.

"You're incredible," he said, unable to keep the words from bursting out of him.

Amelia's eyes fixed on his and he saw her pupils widen with lust and hunger for him, and he knew he must have been looking back at her in the exact same way.

He took her wine glass from her and placed it down with his own, before the arm her had around her shoulder pulled her closer to him and he held her face with his free hand so he could stare deeply into her eyes, their lips only millimeters apart.

"I've been waiting my whole life for a woman like you," he whispered as his dragon began to roar inside of him.

Her eyes seemed so open and engorged, and he stroked the side of her face with his thumb and pulled her in ever so slightly, so their lips grazed against each other and he felt her tremble and heard her gasp. He could hear her heart pounding, and he could smell her arousal. She was willing to open for him like a flower, but he had to be careful with her, she was delicate, and he was so powerful, and she didn't yet know what he truly was.

She bit her bottom lip nervously and he could sense how

much she wanted him, it was palpable. Her heart was pounding so fast and her skin was prickling with desire and heat. When he finally leaned in and put them both out of their misery, he kissed her long and hard on the mouth, taking her breath away as she moaned and leaned into him. She slowly let her arms come up and wrap around his neck, holding him there as they passionately embraced and kissed each other, exploring each other with their tongues in what was the culmination of all the tension that had been between them since the very moment they had almost bumped into each other outside of the B&B.

When they finally broke apart, Dash gasped too, he felt as if his soul had been stirred so much that he was standing on the edge of a cliff, about to throw himself off into the unknown. He looked deeply into her eyes and knew that it was meant to be, but also that he was on dangerous ground.

Could his heart handle it?

She smiled and stroked his neck with her fingers as she stared into his eyes.

"I want to be with you," she whispered, and he could see the look in her eyes. The naughty glint of longing, the desire for him to take her to bed and make her his.

And he wanted that too, more than anything. But he had to tread carefully. To unleash his dragon on her without her knowing, could be a disaster. And he was falling deep for this woman, he was certain she was his fated mate. He had to be cautious.

He rose to his feet and pulled her with him, when she felt his power she gasped, and he could hear her heart pounding away in her chest. He found his eyes travelling to where it lay beneath the skin, his dragon stirred even more, his cock pulsing in his jeans, getting harder by the second.

God, he wanted her.

And it made it even harder for him to know that she wanted him so badly too.

He kissed her again, their lips meeting in a total frenzy, before he scooped her up effortlessly in his arms and began to carry her as he walked toward the hallway, out of the kitchen and living area and into the main entrance hall. The huge chandelier glinted over their heads as he began to walk up the stairs, one by one.

At the section where they split, he went to the right and into his side of the house. His huge master bedroom was already lit with lowlights and the gas fire was burning in the corner of the room. It felt so romantic, and it hadn't even been intended. It was all like it was meant to be, and the flames casting fiery light around the room only made it more perfect.

He stepped close to the bed and lay her down, their eyes locked in on each other's as he slowly began to remove her clothes. He pulled her jeans off slowly, teasing them off as she arched her back and moaned as he leaned in over her and began to trail kisses up her stomach.

When she was only in her underwear and was laid out in front of him like an offering, he took hold of her by the ankle and kissed her there, before trailing kisses up her thighs.

"I need you," she gasped as he moved up higher.

He growled, his dragon coming to the surface, and he saw the expression on her face change. For a moment there was fear, before the lust took her over again.

"There's still so much you need to know," he whispered.

She arched her back as he slipped his hands into her underwear and pulled down her panties before he tossed them over his shoulder onto the floor. When he picked up her legs and moved his face down between her thighs, he could feel her tense up — until he ran his tongue over her and she exploded into moans and groans.

As he licked and ate her, he tasted her sweet juices and felt her heat rising. The dragon inside of him was desperate to claim her, and he felt his energy go into her, it possessed her and was taking her over. When she came hard and heavy, she grabbed hold of his head and he took as much of her cunt into his mouth as he could as she bucked her hips and quivered. He was so hard and wanted so badly to fuck her, but he had to honor her. He had to wait.

After she stopped panting and writhing around on the sheets, Dash climbed up beside her and wrapped her up in his arms. He knew she would be exhausted... even though she didn't know it yet, having a dragon go down on her would have taken all her energy, and he watched as she quickly fell asleep in his arms.

He smiled and kissed her on the neck.

He did love her already, he knew he did.

She was so incredible, and now, he had shown her an animalistic part of him that would either terrify or excite her.

He just hoped it was the latter.

CHAPTER 11

*A*melia woke to the sensation of being wrapped up on a soft, fluffy cloud. The comfort was enveloping her, making her drift between asleep and awake, and as if she were drifting through space.

She had never been this comfortable or rested in her entire life. The blanket and pillows she was using, the mattress they were lying on, all of it was another level of bliss. When she finally worked up the courage to open her eyes and potentially break the spell, she was stunned for a moment as she had to work out where she was.

She sat up slowly and looked around the room, only to see the fire still burning away in the corner, the wonderful view of the pine trees out the window, and the deep rooted knowledge within her that she was in Dash's bed. She smiled and the memory started to come back to her. The kiss, the incredible kiss.

Not just on her lips, but somewhere else too.

She felt herself begin to blush. What a night it had been.

She had had the most intense orgasm of her life, and she

had felt something change between her and Dash too. He had done something to her. Something very exciting and intense.

She reluctantly swung her legs out of bed and rose to her feet, only to find that her whole body felt different. It was as if she had been reborn, her eyes felt wide and sparkling, her heart was beating with purpose, and she had the sensation rocketing through her that her blood was powerful and new. She was full of energy, and she felt so satisfied and overtaken by pleasure, as if she has been released and then left to float to the ground, landing on soft feathers.

In short, she had never felt this damned good in her whole life.

She saw her clothes had been moved to a chair by the large French doors that overlooked the back garden and the pine trees beyond. She scooped them up and dressed quickly, her newfound energy helping her each step of the way. She felt strong and capable, and completely different to how she had felt when she woke up the morning before.

And Dash… Oh My… Dash… she thought.

She had fallen for him now, and she knew there was no turning back. He had wanted her the same as she had wanted him… and he had taken charge of her body and shown her what intense passion and love could be like.

She wandered out of the bedroom and around the gallery landing, her mind had been in such a swirl of passion and desire when he had carried her to the bedroom she barely remembered getting there. And it was as if she were seeing this part of the house for the first time. The right side of the staircase, Dash's side, with his incredible master suite, office, and games room.

She went down the stairs slowly and couldn't believe it when she saw the clock on the wall said it was almost noon. She had slept for almost twelve hours. She picked up her pace, expecting to walk into the kitchen and see it empty, but her instinct kicked in and it took her by surprise. She felt the pull of him, and she knew he was near.

Dash was waiting for her in the kitchen, he was standing, leaning back against the counter, sipping a cup of coffee, and looking rugged and so damned good she didn't quite know what to do with herself. She felt something ignite within her, something animalistic.

She faltered and his eyes moved up to meet hers, a wry smile playing on his lips.

"Good morning," he said with amusement. "Or should I say…"

"Afternoon?" she interjected and smiled at him knowingly.

"You needed to sleep," he said. "It was to be expected."

The sentence surprised her. She didn't know what he meant by it exactly, but she could only figure that it had something to do with how she was feeling. As if she had been changed somehow, deep inside of her.

She looked at him and cocked her head to the side, and she suddenly noticed that he had cooked for them both. She had been so busy looking at him she had barely noticed the delicious brunch laid out on the island before him.

"Wow," she said. "That all looks very, very good."

She moved closer, and Dash reached out and wrapped his arms around her. He pulled her up against him, and she felt his taught muscles beneath his t-shirt. She reached up and ran her hands through his hair and down to his beard before he kissed her hard on the mouth. Her whole body responded to him, and the memory of him and what he had done to her the night before made her nerve endings tingle. She wanted him all over again, to feel his mouth against her pussy, to feel his hot and heavy tongue flicking up and down her and making her crash into that wave of pleasure.

She was almost panting, and when their lips broke apart and he stared into his eyes he saw he had a passionate look in his too.

"Last night," she whispered.

Dash nodded.

"It was incredible," he said. "You were incredible."

She smiled meekly and then as he slipped his hand into hers and led her back to the island so they could sit and he could serve her brunch, she realized how at home she was with him there. She truly felt as if this home was beginning to become hers too. As if they were already slipping into family life.

"Did Nora go to school okay?" she asked.

Dash nodded as he put the plunger down in the coffee and began to pour Amelia a cup.

"She did," he smiled. "She's looking forward to heading up to the golf resort later for Kid's Club."

"I'm looking forward to seeing it too," Amelia admitted. "It sounds lovely from what you've told me."

"It's good for the town," he said as he began to present different plates of gorgeous-looking food. Bacon, pancakes, fresh fruit, syrup, pastries and preserves. "We need to keep this place sparkling and with high standards so that we keep attracting tourists. Winter is usually our busiest time when ski season has fully kicked in at its height and people come to spend the holidays here at cabins. A lot of wealthy families from all over the country have their own properties here and are members of the golf resort year-round too, but we get a lot of new folks coming to town for a one-off year. Some lease the mountain log cabins or bigger houses and stay throughout Christmas and New Year's. It really is a magical time around here."

"I bet it's amazing," she said. "It's so picturesque anyway, but when it's fully covered in snow and twinkling lights, I can imagine it is even more stunning."

Dash smiled and sat next to her. She felt as if they had completely eased into each other's company, and now that they had broken the sexual tension between them she didn't feel as if she had to avoid his gaze anymore for fear of giving herself away. But she could tell that he was still holding back on something, and the way that she felt so amazing and reborn was also making her wonder what was going on.

Who was this man, really? And what had he done to her?

Before she had chance to open her mouth to broach the subject, Dash suddenly turned slightly toward her and took a deep breath.

"There's something I need to tell you," he said quickly, as if the words had been trying to fight their way out of him for days.

Amelia felt her stomach drop with nerves and her mouth instantly went dry. She could see the look on his face, as if he were very nervous and she could only assume that this would not be good news.

"Okay…" she said, her hands shaking a little. The last thing she wanted was for him to break it off with her before things had even really begun.

What could he be about to say?

Her mind instantly started to work on overtime, and in what could have only been a maximum of three seconds she had already thought of many possible scenarios…

He was actually married to Nora's mom, and she was coming back… or, he didn't want to commit right now and therefore last night had been fun but it wouldn't be happening again… or, he felt as if things were becoming too complicated and he was going to have to fire her…

Amelia's heart was pounding out of her chest and she was wracked with nerves.

When he finally reached over and took hold of her hands, she felt a rush of electricity rocket between them again and it made her calm. She looked into his eyes and saw a fire burning in them slowly and gently and it was as if she had been put into a trance. She was completely at ease and her nerves were vanishing.

"I have a secret," Dash said cautiously. "But after last night, and after all that I have been feeling with you, I need to tell you before we can truly go any further."

"Okay," she said, urging him to continue.

"This is going to feel like a lot," he said. "But after our conversation last night about Misty Vale and all the legends that swirl around this town, I hope that is may make it a little easier to digest."

Amelia looked into his eyes and saw the fire burning brightly right in the center, as if it were a part of him. Her pulse thumped harder and she felt as if she were on the verge of understanding something. She thought of the way she was when he was around, as if they were already joined from the moment they had met.

"I told you there were legends of vampires and fairies and men who could turn themselves into animals…" he said slowly.

Amelia nodded, her eyes wide.

"It isn't myth or just legend," he said. "They truly do exist… right here in Misty Vale. Throughout the entire world in fact… but here, we have a concentrated group of the paranormal… and well…" he took a deep breath and sighed. "I am part of it."

As soon as he had said it, she knew it was all coming together. Ideas were forming in her mind, and connections were being made. The heat that powered through him, the animalistic nature that seemed to take him over, the power and the poise he held at all times unless she and he were locked in a moment of lust. There was something else running through his veins, something so powerful she had yet to experience it… but she wanted to. She wanted to know it all.

"I'm a dragon shifter Amelia," Dash said, breaking her mad thoughts. "I can turn into a dragon."

She felt stunned into silence.

A dragon shifter? She had never heard of one of those.

Werewolves, yes… but a dragon?

She seemed to lean back slightly, and she exhaled. She felt as if she had been holding her breath for an hour, and suddenly with the revelation of his words, it was as if she finally dared to again.

A DRAGON SHIFTER.

She paused and looked into his eyes. She could see he was searching her expression for an answer and she didn't know what the hell to say.

"The fire in your eyes, I've seen it…" was all she could manage. "And I feel the heat on you. Last night it went into me."

Dash nodded.

"What did you do to me?" she asked, barely daring to hear the answer. Would she turn into a dragon now too? Or had he just given her some of his power?

"I loved you," he said. "Since the moment we set eyes on each other something powerful happened between us, you must have felt it?"

"I did," she said.

She wasn't afraid, but her mind was scrambled. This was a lot to take in, he was right about that one.

"When my kind find the person that they are meant to be with, their fated and on true mate, something happens. It's called imprinting."

Amelia was sure she had heard that term somewhere

before, maybe in romance book she had read or on television, but she had never in her wildest dreams thought it was something that could be real. And yet, here she was experiencing it first-hand.

"Our souls connected that day outside the B&B when you had just arrived in town," he continued. "One look, one meet of our eyes, one brief touch, that was all it took, and it set something off. A chain of events that would be impossible to break or overcome."

"Wow…" she whispered, her mind was being blown, but it all made perfect sense. She had been able to feel his gaze on her ever since that moment outside when he had almost knocked her over, and she had thought about nothing but him since. He had come into her mind and dominated her thoughts, she had dreamt about it, longed for him, been brought closer to him by what seemed like fate. And now, she had given part of her body to him, and also her heart.

"We are meant to be together," Dash said. "But for us to truly be together, I wanted you to know what I was and why this was happening. It is a lot to take in… and for us to be together properly, for our bodies to be joined, it's a big step."

She felt herself blush a little at the thought of her making love with a dragon. A man who had that beast hidden inside of him.

"Are you dangerous?" she asked.

"No," he smiled. "Well, not to you."

She felt a wave of relief.

"But I am powerful, and for me to claim you… when we are together on that level, it is a life changing experience, one that will seal us together for the rest of time."

She was so confused, and yet at the same time it was all making perfect sense. Her mind was blown, and this was not what she had been expecting when she had met Dash and come to Misty Vale, and yet she was being swept up in it and she was enjoying every second.

"I'm your protector now," Dash said as he squeezed her hand tightly in reassurance. "I'll always know if you are in danger or any trouble, and I can be there in a heartbeat right by your side."

She smiled and looked deeply into his eyes.

"This is all so... magic..." she said breathlessly.

"It is," he said. "But it is real... very, very real."

She nodded and let him come closer to her, he wrapped his arms around her and pulled her up against his chest. Knowing that he had a dragon beneath his skin, lurking somewhere and ready to break free was as exciting as it was terrifying. But she knew she could handle it. Dash was right, this was something bigger than fear or excitement. Their bond and their connection were out of this world, it was something neither of them could have predicted and neither of them could now deny.

She looked up into his eyes and saw the glint of fire there, the special part of him that made him oh so very different, and she wrapped her arms around his neck. He leaned in and kissed her, and knowing what he was now, she felt herself give herself over to him truly. Their kiss felt deeper and more passionate, as if now that the secret had been told, they would be able to move forward without apprehension or fear.

She felt as if she knew the true him, the real him, and it made her even more unable to understand how and why Nora's mother had walked out on them. But it was clear that he could never have had a connection like this with her. This was something that only happened once in a lifetime.

When their kiss ended, she smiled and they just held each other, standing there in the middle of the kitchen, embraced, and falling completely in love.

It had been the most unexpected development in their relationship for her, and yet it was one that was so right. For her, she had always had an open mind and she knew she was the right person to move forward and take this in her stride.

Dash, her dragon… she felt like the luckiest woman in the world.

CHAPTER 12

The golf resort was busy later that day as Dash, Amelia and Nora stepped inside.

It was a hive of activity, one that Dash was very proud of and that he and his family had spent a lot of money, time and passion making something special for Misty Vale. He watched as Amelia took it all in, he knew that this place was something else, and it was an impressive feeling as you first walked through the door.

Dash showed them all through to the club room and they took a table overlooking the green. Some golfers were still out there in the distance with their carts and caddy's, and Dash felt the urge himself to head out and hit the fairway, but that would have to wait. He had much more important things to attend to. Amelia for one.

"Kids club is opening in five minutes," Dash said as he looked at his watch. "Why don't we let Amelia sit here and I take you over?"

"Are you sure?" Amelia asked.

He could see that she looked a little worried, as if she thought she should be the one running around after Nora, and while she was still the nanny, Dash wanted her to know that he didn't want her to feel that way. He was her father and he wanted them to just be there together as a three as well.

Dash winked at her and took Nora's hand as he walked out of the club room and toward the entrance of Kid's Club. He looked back over his shoulder as he went and looked at Amelia as she stared out at the green and he felt a real surge of adoration for her. It felt so good to have her here at one of the main hubs of his life, where his family and business collided on such a grand level.

Once Nora was safely dropped off to spend the next couple of hours playing, crafting and doing sports, Dash made his way back to Amelia and found her sitting almost exactly like she hadn't moved a muscle, in a trance, looking out over part of the green.

"I've never played golf," she said as he sat back down, letting her concentration be broken. "How far does the course go?"

"It goes on for miles," Dash smiled. "It's so big, out in every direction, but when you walk around the full course it's a damned good days exercise," he laughed.

"The view is so stunning too, with the mountains in the background," she smiled. "Really spectacular."

"When we made the decision to develop this section of land, that was one of the main things we wanted to make sure we kept, the incredible view from right here," he said as he pointed his finger down on the table. "We knew this clubhouse had to be extra special, with the open aspects and all the glass."

"It certainly has the wow factor," she smiled.

"I just wish everyone in town appreciated it," he said.

"What do you mean? How could they not?" Amelia cocked her head to the side.

Dash leaned in a little across the table and lowered his voice. There were plenty of people in the club room both dining and socializing, but he wanted to make sure he wasn't heard in any way.

"Well, with regards to what I told you earlier, with the legends…"

Amelia nodded.

"There aren't just dragons, vampires and fairies…" he said. "There's also a bear family, and over the years I guess things between my pack and theirs haven't always been peaceful."

"Oh really?" Amelia asked, her eyebrows going up high. "Tell me more."

Dash smiled and laughed.

"The bears are not very much like us," he continued. "They don't go in for all this kind of thing. Their businesses haven't been as lucrative as ours, shall we say, and I think they believe part of the reason for that is because of something that happened a long, long time ago. Back in the first years of the town being founded."

"And they're still bothered?" Amelia asked with confusion.

"This is a small town," Dash said with a shrug. "And we have two very different types of animal here… I mean, bears and dragons…"

Amelia nodded, it was clear she hadn't really thought of the full implications.

"At the moment, things are peaceful enough, but I don't know… I feel as if something may be brewing. As if it would only take one small thing to set off a war."

"Jesus," she looked worried, and Dash felt the need to reassure her…

"I mean, this is just the way things are. I guess a bit like two gangs who don't often see eye to eye, but like I say, we tend to keep out of each other's way, and then we can all coexist without too much trouble."

Amelia nodded. He could tell that she understood.

"And what about these vampires and fairies?" she asked excitedly. "Do I need to be looking over my shoulder at night? Avoiding certain places after dark? I mean a vampire sounds pretty scary!"

Dash smiled and shook his head.

"The vampire we have here is one of the good guys… but his brother… well, he wasn't. He spent some time terrorizing a town a couple of hundred miles from here called Bridge Hollow. But we won't get into that."

"And the fairy?" she asked.

"The fairy…" Dash thought for a moment. "Well, I don't know a whole lot about her. There is only one as far as I know, and it's the lady who runs the magic shop on Main Street."

"A magic shop?" Amelia sat forward with an excited look. "I don't think I've seen that place yet."

"Oh, it's there, you just need to know where to look," Dash winked. "I think she fronts it as a quirky gift store… but once you're inside, there is magic to be found."

He said it ominously and with fun, and Amelia laughed.

"She's been here for over a hundred years," he said. "And she's barely aged. She only looks to be in her early forties now."

"Wow," Amelia said. "That is incredible."

"I told you Misty Vale was full of secrets and surprises," Dash smiled.

"I'm starting to truly understand that," she agreed.

He reached over and took hold of her hand, and at the exact same time he noticed over her shoulder that Striker and Zane, two of his fellow dragon brothers, had walked in.

"Well," Dash smiled. "Two of my brothers have just arrived and I would love for you to meet them."

He had told them little about Amelia, but he knew that they would both be able to tell that he had imprinted on her and that she was his. He had let them know he was hiring a nanny to look after their niece Nora, but he knew his brothers, and the second they saw Amelia and the way Dash was with her, they were going to know that she was something special.

He wondered how they would respond to the revelation, and he felt quite excited by it.

"Brother," Zane said as he approached the table and held out his arm and hand.

Dash rose to his feet and the pair gripped their fists together and then came in for an embrace.

"My brother," Dash said.

He greeted Striker too, and then he stood back and watched as their eyes travelled down to Amelia before they went straight back up to Dash.

"And who is this?" Striker asked with a warm smile.

Amelia looked nervous, and Dash had to admit it would likely be a lot for her to take in. She had learned a lot today, and suddenly she was being thrown into the deep end with three powerful dragon brothers.

"Hello," she smiled, as she held out her hand. "I'm Amelia."

Dash was impressed, she could certainly hold her own and not look phased. She was continuing to surprise him and surpass expectations.

Striker smiled and shook her hand and when his skin connected with hers, Dash instantly saw the look of under-standing and recognition spread out across his face. He could sense from touching Amelia's skin that she had been imprinted on. That she was taken, and Striker looked at Dash with wide eyes and smiled.

"Amelia," he said, still holding Dash's stare. "It is an absolute pleasure to meet you."

Dash felt proud, and as if he had something over them now. Both Striker and Zane had yet to find their other halves, they were still waiting for a lightning bolt to strike them and for their lives to be changed. Even if neither of them would admit it.

"Amelia," Zane said as he reached out and shook her hand.

Zane's eyes flicked up instantly to meet Dash's and he smirked.

"Well, well, well…" he said. "I wasn't expecting any of this today."

"You know me," Dash said. "I'm full of surprises."

He watched Amelia shift uncomfortably in her seat, as if she didn't understand what was happening and it brought him back into the moment with her. Of course, she was going to be confused, and he didn't want her to feel weird about it.

"Why don't you join us," Dash said. "Nora is in Kid's Club and we were just about to have a drink."

"Well we would," Striker said. "But really we have a lot going on, we hoped we would find you here and be able to catch you quick."

"Okay," Dash said, his nerves momentarily rising. He could tell that something was wrong, and he wanted to know immediately. He looked down at Amelia to check that she was doing okay, but she looked calm and at ease, eagerly listening to what was about to be said.

"These bikers that have been spotted around town," Striker began. "We did some digging and we've found out who they are. They're from further west, a group called the Forsaken Riders. It looks like they've come to town with an interest in the Oktoberfest that is happening in a few weeks' time."

Now this was interesting.

Dash cocked his head to the side and listened.

"We don't know yet what they're planning, if anything at all, but obviously a gang sniffing around our town isn't something we want to ignore. I think it's best that we stay on top of the situation."

Dash nodded.

"Most certainly," he said. "Do we know what they're doing here so far?"

"No," Zane said, interjecting. "But I have reason to believe that they have been spotted with some of the bears. As if maybe they know them already or they are just getting to know them now."

"The bears organize the Oktoberfest," Dash said. "Could it be business related?"

"Sure," Striker said with a shrug. "But do we really want a gang coming into our town and starting up business alliances with the bears?"

This was a predicament, they didn't want the bears gaining any beneficial business deals over them, it just wouldn't be good for the dragons in any way. They needed to get a handle on all of this and fast.

"I don't like the sound of this," Dash said. "We need to get to these bikers, we need to speak with them somehow and find out what their true interest is here and why."

"Agreed," said Striker.

Dash looked down at Amelia who was watching them all with interest, and he reached over and touched her hand. She turned hers over so their fingers could connect, and he felt so grateful to have her there with him.

He sensed his brothers look at each other, and when he looked over at them, he could see that they were pleased at these most recent developments with him and Amelia. A dragon finding his mate was an exciting event, and they would no doubt be able to see the change within him.

"Well, thanks for finding me and letting me know," Dash said. "At least we are on top of things and ahead of the game. We can find out what is happening soon enough I'm sure. And hopefully, put things right."

Striker and Zane agreed before they rose to their feet and they all took turns to hug. They then turned to Amelia and smiled at her warmly.

"Welcome to Misty Vale Amelia," Zane said. "I think you're going to be very, very happy here."

When his brothers had gone, he looked at her and she was smiling. He could sense her happiness and it was only making him feel even better too.

They really had found something special, and now that she had met his two most powerful blood brothers and they had approved, he knew that things could only get better from here.

CHAPTER 13

*A*fter a whirlwind few days, Amelia finally found herself back at the B&B flopping down onto her bed and sighing a very satisfied sigh. She had never been this happy before, and she loved the fact that she had settled into Misty Vale life so well.

Now, she had a day or two where she wasn't going to be nannying Nora, but she still was going to be spending time with them, Dash had already said he didn't want her to go too far.

She loved the fact that he was so protective over her, and everything she had learned about the town and its supernatural residents had only made things even more intense. She breathed in deep and smiled.

How could she ever have seen any of this coming?

She rolled over and grabbed her cellphone and tapped it to life and noticed that she had a text message from Jane, the young lady in the beauty parlor who had given her a pamper and spruce up.

J: Hey Girl! It's the freaking weekend, fancy getting that night out? I can show you what Misty Vale is all about xx

Amelia smiled and began to type her reply. She did deserve a night out after all the work she had been doing and all the stuff that had happened to her over the past few years, what with Toby and his obsessive control.

A: That sounds like a great plan! How about tonight? Xx

She had only hit send and a few seconds had passed when she had a reply.

J: Perfect! I'll swing by the B&B around 8? See you then! X

Amelia grinned and held her phone to her chest. A new man, a new job, and now a girl's night out on the horizon. Life in Misty Vale was pretty damn perfect.

She jumped up and walked over to her closet, looking inside, and scanning all the clothes she had in there. She didn't have a whole lot that was suitable for a wild night in a club, but a few drinks around some of the local bars, she could probably manage.

She moved her pants around on the hangers and settled on some skinny jeans that she could wear with some high boots, she also chose a black tight t-shirt, some earrings and her new cute leather jacket with the fur collar.

She laid them all out on the bed and then she reached for her phone again and started to call Dash. He answered on only the second ring.

"Hey there," he said smoothly, his voice was like silk and it made Amelia's bones quiver.

"Hey," she said, feeling a heat creep up her chest. She wanted to be with him, to hold him again. She couldn't shake him from her thoughts, and it was so hard.

"It's been almost a full ten hours since I've seen you," he said. And Amelia couldn't help but be brought back to that morning when she had woken up in his arms, completely wiped out from a night of passion. They still hadn't sealed their union officially, but Dash was very good with his tongue… and Amelia couldn't get enough.

"It's been a long ten hours," she said mischievously. "I've been missing you."

"Me too," he said. "I'm still at work, but I'm looking forward to finishing up and getting home. How are things at the B&B?"

"All okay," she said. "It's quite nice coming back for a little while to sort out my things, I feel like I have emails to catch up on and laundry."

"You can always bring your laundry here," he said. "You can spend as much time in the house as you need, you don't need to wait until you're heading home with Nora."

"Are you sure?" she asked.

"Of course, I'm sure," he half laughed. "I'll take care of you."

She smiled and felt warm inside. She liked it when he talked like that. It made her feel so loved and appreciated.

"Well, thank you," she said. "I will definitely take you up on that."

"Good," he said. "No point in you clashing down to the laundromat with your things when I have a super laundry room right here that is barely ever in use."

She laughed. She could only imagine.

"So, I've just been speaking to Jane," she said. "You know the lady who runs one of the beauty and hair salons on Main Street?"

"I think so," he said. "I'm sure I would recognize her anyway."

"Well, we're going to go for a few drinks tonight," she said as she pinned the phone to her ear using her shoulder and looked through her make-up bag. "She offered to show me around to some of the bars and I quote "What Misty Vale is all about."" She laughed, and Dash did a little too.

"Oh, well, that sounds fun," he said, but she was sure she

could hear a tinge of something in his voice, as if he didn't truly feel that way. "I'm sure you'll enjoy exploring."

"I haven't been in a bar for over two years pretty much, so I'm sure I'll find it interesting if nothing else. But it'll be nice to see Jane."

"Sure," he said.

There was a pause and Amelia felt a little worried, was he angry with her? Or was she just overreacting and expecting that of him because it's something Toby would do? She thought for a moment, if this was Toby, then he would have screamed at her down the phone and called her all sorts of names, and then he would have turned up and physically forbid her from leaving the house. She had to be overthinking.

"What are you and Nora up to tonight?" she asked to break the silence.

"Well, once I've finished up here at the office I'm going to collect her from school, take her across to the golf club quickly for some dinner and then I thought I would bring her home for a movie and an early night. She's exhausted at the moment, I think all the excitement of having you around has kept her up so late she needs to catch up." He laughed and so did Amelia.

"She has been going to bed pretty late," Amelia smiled. "But it has been so lovely just all being together."

"It really has," Dash said, his voice warm. "So, I guess I'll see you tomorrow?" he asked.

"I'd love that," Amelia grinned. "Even though I'm officially off the clock."

"There's no clock anymore," Dash mused. "I just want you to feel at home here."

"Oh, I do," she said.

"Good," he laughed. "We'll have a good evening with Jane, and I will text you later on."

"Okay, babe," she smiled. "Give my love to Nora, and I'll see you both tomorrow."

"See you tomorrow babe," he said, and then she ended the call.

She sat back on the bed and smiled, but something was nagging at her. She was sure that as soon as she had said she was going out with Jane his tone had changed slightly. But he had still been so loving, maybe she had imagined it.

She felt cross at herself for being so paranoid and tried to shake it off. She had to stop self-sabotaging… Dash was not Toby.

She shook her head, jumped to her feet, and headed toward the bathroom. It may have only been midafternoon, but this woman wanted to take her time getting ready and enjoying every moment. She may even treat herself to something from the mini bar if she was feeling fancy enough.

She laughed and turned on the shower, when she stepped under the warm water she felt as if she were being completely revived again after the intensity of the past week. She had spent so much time with Dash, and her body was exhausted, but his power still throbbed through her and was making her feel more alive.

Once she had finished, got out and dried and moisturized, she sat down at the desk and started to do her make-up. She had never enjoyed doing it until recently, she had always had this stigma surrounding how she felt because of her mother, but today she was going to enjoy getting dolled up and going to meet her friend. Dash had seen her both with and without make-up and he had always made her feel beautiful. It was so encouraging to feel that and to feel wanted and adored.

She just wished she could shake the nagging sense of doubt that he hadn't liked the idea she was going out with Jane. She scowled at her reflection and tried not to let it take her over. She couldn't let herself feel dark like that, she was all about the light now. The darkness of her past was firmly shut away.

* * *

By the time it was approaching 8pm, Amelia had had so much fun getting ready, doing her make-up, styling her new and improved hair, having a cheeky mini bottle of wine from the very old mini-bar in the bedroom and listening to music as she danced and got herself even more in the mood.

She had thrown the curtains open wide and let the view of the mountains take her through to the end of the day, she had watched it go dark slowly and as all the little twinkling lights had started to pop up over the mountainside. She really did love it here. She was starting to feel as if it was impossible that she had ever lived anywhere else.

She put on her boots and slipped on her jacket before she had one more spritz of perfume and grabbed her handbag. She would wander down to the lobby, say hello to Maude and wait for Jane to arrive.

Downstairs, it was quite busy as a few people were checking in after a coach had just rolled into town. Amelia smiled and waved at Maude, and as she turned around, she saw that Jane was bouncing through the doors with a massive smile on her face.

"Wow!" she beamed. "Look at you! You look like a million dollars!"

"Why thank you," Amelia smiled. "You look fantastic yourself."

The two women hugged in greeting and then they headed straight back for the double doors and out into the night.

It was the first time that Amelia had properly been out on Main Street late when it had been so busy and full of people clearly heading out to have fun. It was wonderful to see how little groups of tourists, or romantic couples, even some that were clearly younger groups of skiers were all making their way to some of the bars or to the restaurants for dinner.

"So, where are we heading?" Amelia asked Jane, who had her arm linked with hers as they wandered along and past some of the bars.

"On a night like tonight, the best place on Main Street is a little bar called Archer's… it's a sports bar and will be full of music and fun, plus the beer is pretty good too."

"Oh, I see it," Amelia smiled and pointed up ahead to a wooden building that had been made to look like a log cabin on the outside. There was a large blue sign over the door that simply said ARCHERS, and already from where they were walking Amelia could hear the music and the chatter of a large crowd coming from inside.

Jane approached and pushed open the door, and when they both stepped inside Amelia felt a wave of relief wash over her. This felt good. The whole place was full of warmth and cheer, and she smiled as she looked at the rich wooden tones that enveloped the walls and the tables. There were pool tables on one side of the room, a jukebox next to them playing out a random selection of songs, a long bar that ran down almost the full width of the main room and lots of booths and tables on the outside of the room and in the center. It felt like a real bar. The kind of one she hadn't been in for some time. Jane led her over to the counter and they sat up on the high stools and just being there was making Amelia so happy she couldn't take the grin from her face. She felt as if she had regained another part of her, and it was wonderful.

"What can I get you ladies?" the bar tender said as he approached them and slung a bar mop over his shoulder.

"Well, I'd love some sparkling wine… what do you think

Amelia?" Jane asked as she placed her purse down on the counter and smiled.

"Perfect," Amelia grinned. "I don't think I could stomach any beer."

The bar tender nodded and headed away to one of the refrigerators.

"That's Archer himself," Jane said in between chews of gum. "He owns this place, obviously, and his family are a founding one too. Misty Vale has all this history, it's pretty wild."

"Oh really?" Amelia asked with wide eyes as her gaze traveled to the bar tender. "I'm learning a bit about it, actually," she continued, but she didn't want to say too much. She had her loyalty to her man, her dragon, and she didn't know if Jane had any idea of what was going on in her town. Dash had said that it was all just thought to be legend, so without Jane hinting that she knew anything more than that, then Amelia was going to stay quiet.

Archer returned with a bottle and two glasses and when he popped the cork Jane gave a little cheer and clapped her hands. The ladies poured themselves a drink and settled into chatting. It felt so good to be out and about with a friend.

"So how has everything been going?" Jane asked with raised brows. "What's it like working for the elusive Dash Livingstone?"

Amelia couldn't help but grin. She tried to hide it, but it was going to be impossible. It was so strange to hear people talking about Dash like this, he seemed to be infamous in Misty Vale, and whereas this had initially made him super intimidating, now she knew the real him and all that came with it, it just made her love him more.

"It's been pretty good," she said with a nod. "I can't complain."

Jane had a suspicious look on her face.

"That sounds to me like you may have been doing a lot more than nannying," she teased.

"Dash is pretty incredible," Amelia said. "I've never been this happy before."

Jane gasped a little and then a wide smile spread across her face.

"Oh my god," she said as she clapped her hands together again. "This is wild. And also, how lucky are you, he's like Misty Vale's most eligible bachelor. Although, I have to say, most people around here find him pretty scary."

"Oh, he can be," Amelia said with a laugh. "But once you really get to know him… there's much more to him than that. I think the word I'm probably looking for is misunderstood, but at the same time, it would be foolish to ever underestimate him… he's very powerful."

"Oh hell, I'll bet!" Jane laughed. "Damn girl, you are lucky!"

Amelia smiled coyly and nodded. She couldn't pretend she didn't feel that way, even if she still had the feeling that he was wasn't happy about her going out nagging at her.

"Well, I think we should drink to that!" said Jane.

The ladies grabbed their glasses and chinked them together.

"To the start of a wonderful night," Jane said. "And to many more to come."

*D*ash was lounging in his office, sipping whiskey, and going over land proposals for a potential new hotel to be built in Misty Vale, when his phone started to blow up.

Zane's name exploded onto the screen again and again with a flurry of messages, and when he reached for it to read them, he didn't even get a chance to tap them open before he was being called by Striker.

"Hey brother," he said. "What's up?"

"Well," Striker said with an ominous tone. "It appears our biker friends have been getting into bed with the bears when it comes to business."

Dash felt his dragon stir and rage. It was not what he had wanted to hear, and now they were going to have to do something about it.

"What are they planning?" he asked. "And do we know any more about them?"

"As far as I can tell, they came to town after hearing about the Oktoberfest, but it looks as if they've been having business meetings with Archer and some of the other bears.

Maybe they're going to have a hand in running it this year, but what I don't like is the fact that it seems to be secretive. We should set up a meeting with the bikers, see if we can get them onside for some of our work too, see what they're really all about."

"Agreed," said Dash. "There's no harm in testing the waters, seeing what sort of business they're in."

"Exactly," Striker said.

They ended the call and Dash felt shaken up. He hadn't had a great day when it had come to his emotions, even though he didn't like to go there too often. Amelia was doing things to him, and he had fallen for her so fast and hard, it felt as if his old hurts were starting to force their way to the surface. His ex-girlfriend, Nora's mother, had been such a party girl that it had ultimately been the thing that had lured her away. He knew Amelia was just having a drink with a local girl around town, and he didn't want to appear, in any way, fazed, but it had awoken something in him, and made him remember old pains, as much as he hated to admit it even to himself.

"You're a fucking moron," he breathed to himself as he held the phone under his chin.

But this stuff with the bears was starting to weigh heavily on him too. How was he going to deal with a potential blow up between the two shifter clans of Misty Vale? They had lived with a known peace for some years now, but it had always been on shaky ground. With his new life with Amelia unfolding, his daughter, and all of his businesses, it felt as if he had the weight of the world bearing down on him.

He sighed, and then his phone started to ring again, and he looked down to see Amelia's name. He smiled.

"Hey there, babe," he said warmly as he answered. "How is girls' night?"

He could hear the sound of music in the background, but

it was as if Amelia were slightly removed from it, like she was in the bathroom or out on the street taking a breather.

"Hey, babe," she said. "It's going good, Jane is a really nice girl. I can see myself making a great friend in her."

Dash smiled, he liked hearing that. He knew it must be so hard for Amelia moving to a new place and trying to start all over again. To know that she had a friend she could turn to would make all the difference and hopefully, lead on to her getting to know more people around town.

"She sounds it," he said. "It's really good of her to take you under her wing and show you around."

"I agree," Amelia answered. "We just seemed to click, it's been a while since I've had so much fun with a friend. How is your night? How is Nora?"

Dash smiled, it felt good to have someone who cared about them. Sure, he had his brothers in arms, and his parents, but when it came to that extra level of love, the deepest kind there was, it felt so different to have Amelia there and for her to be asking.

"She's good, babe," he said. "She's fast asleep and has been for a few hours now, like we expected, she was exhausted."

"Bless her," Amelia said warmly.

"So, where are you? Which famous Misty Vale haunt did Jane take you to?" Dash asked. "It sounds like there's a good atmosphere?"

"We're in a bar called Archer's," Amelia replied. "Some sports bar in the middle of Main Street, it's really good! We've just been chatting to the owner."

Dash couldn't help but scowl. Archer Savage was a complete pain in his ass, and one of the bear clan. He felt himself bristle. After the conversation he had just had with Striker, he couldn't help but wonder what the hell was going to happen if they started to get on the wrong side of each other again.

"Archer Savage?" he asked, with clear disdain in his voice. Even if it was unintended.

"Yeah, I think so," Amelia said innocently. "Jane said he was the name above the door."

Dash gritted his teeth and paused, but it was clear that Amelia had noticed, and she'd had a drink and was feeling even more feisty than she normally was.

"You know, I can't help but get the feeling you're being pissy with me because I've come out tonight," she said.

"I'm not being pissy," he replied, rubbing his temples. The anger about Archer rising even more to the surface.

"Yes, you are," she said. "And I want you to know that I won't tolerate it."

Dash felt as if he had been slapped and he sat back in his chair. His mom and his ex-girlfriend had always been women who needed pleasing, and he felt as if he had spent the past week doing nothing but pleasing Amelia; now she was out on the town and not giving a shit. And with none other than Archer fucking Savage.

"Jesus, Amelia," he said with a low breath.

"Well?" she barked down the phone.

This was making his blood boil even more and he could feel the red mist descending.

"Anyway, I'm going to go," she said. "Screw this."

And then, the line went dead.

Dash gritted his teeth again and hurled the phone across the room where it cracked against the wall and the screen shattered. He had never felt rage like it, but he knew it was coming from a place of love. He rose to his feet, knocked back the rest of the whiskey and made his way out of the office and down into the hall.

Maybe he wasn't cut out for another serious relationship. He had gotten so swept up in how he was feeling, in how Amelia had spoken to his soul, that he had completely forgotten how damaged he had become from the events of his past.

As he stormed into his bedroom, all he could smell was Amelia. She seemed to be everywhere, and he closed the door and sighed.

How had he managed to let his emotions get the better of him and fuck it all up so royally?

He went over to the French doors and sat down on the chair and looked out over the starry night above the mountains and the pine forest. He felt his dragon raging away beneath his skin, but he would not succumb to it tonight. He needed to relax and stay calm and he needed to get his head straight.

Because, he had the terrible feeling, he may have just driven Amelia away for good.

CHAPTER 15

*A*melia woke up early the following morning, with not so much as a booze hangover, but a hangover from her fight with Dash.

Her and Jane had had such a good evening. They had sat in Archer's for a couple of hours, before moving on to another bar that was a bit more sophisticated and less raw around the edges. It had big leather chairs, dark lighting, a cocktail menu, and ambient house music playing over the speakers. Amelia had sunk down into the chairs with an espresso martini and wished she could have enjoyed it the way she wanted to, but she had just been consumed by thoughts of Dash.

The fight on the phone had rattled her, and it had come almost out of nowhere. But she had to admit, she had been worrying about it all night before she had called him, and she had wondered whether he was actually mad at her or not. When she had heard the still frosty tone in his voice when they had been speaking, she had just lost it. And now she felt like a fool.

She rolled over and buried her head in the pillows. Her

duvet was so warm and toasty, and she didn't feel as if she ever wanted to get up, but her cellphone was on the other side of the room and she wanted to see if she had any calls or messages from Dash.

She quickly jumped up and ran across to swipe the phone from the desk and climbed back into bed before it even felt as if her feet had truly touched the ground.

She pressed the screen to light it up, but there was nothing there. No calls, no messages, no emails… nothing. She refreshed her emails just to be sure, in the back of her mind she had half been expecting some kind of lengthy apology sent to her in the middle of the night. But he hadn't gotten in touch.

Her stomach dropped and she buried her head in her hands.

"Oh man I've really messed this up," she said, her eyes welling up with tears.

"The most amazing man you've ever met, and you start to worry because his tone is a little different…" she looked across the room and stared into space.

Had she been justified in challenging him? Or had she gone overboard?

The lines felt so blurred for her after her relationship with Toby. She never would have dared challenge him, and she knew how controlling he was… she had just feared that if Dash wasn't pleased about her going out with Jane, then it would spiral. But was he even upset with her about that? She felt herself pout and grow a little irritated.

She thought and thought, but she couldn't get any sense to come into her mind. They had both been on the phone call, and she was just starting to get herself back.

She wasn't going to bend.

She put on her brave face, pulled back the covers and went toward the shower.

Miserable or not, she had a life to live. And she was going to have to get on with it before she let herself slip into her old ways.

* * *

By the time Monday morning had come around, Amelia felt more miserable than ever. Her phone had stayed silent except for some messages from Jane, and she had spent the later part of the weekend pacing around the B&B. She didn't know what she had been expecting but being left to flounder by Dash hadn't been it. And now she was mad. Truly mad.

She had another day off after being so hectic and she wasn't sure back at the Livingstone house with Nora until the following day. It meant she had a whole other day with her thoughts, and she wasn't sure she could handle it. She picked up her coat, slipped it on over her shoulders and headed out to see Jane. Surely, her new best friend could give her some advice.

When she reached the salon she gave a quick recap of what had gone down, from the original phone call when she had told him she was going out with Jane, to later that night when she had nipped outside at Archer's to call him again.

"He sounds like a jerk," Jane said with her arms crossed over her chest and her head shaking from side to side. "How did the argument even escalate?"

"I don't know," Amelia said with her head in her hands. "I called him and I think I was already on edge because of how I was feeling about how he had been earlier, and then suddenly he went quiet on the phone again and I thought he was unhappy because I was out and not sat at home like some good little woman and I snapped."

Jane pouted and sighed. Her arms still firmly fixed across her chest.

"Did he say anything like that though?" she asked, tentatively. "Or did you just assume he was feeling that way."

Amelia tried to remember the conversation in full, but the lines were blurred. All she knew was that she hadn't spoken to him now since the Friday night and her heart was in tatters. She would never admit it to him or to Jane how bad it felt, but she was in turmoil. She had never felt so miserable, they had broken up over something so stupid.

"You told me your ex-boyfriend was controlling and your mom always put the pressure on you to be perfect," Jane said slowly, as if she were testing the water. "Do you think maybe you jumped to conclusions and assumed the worst? I mean, I don't know Dash Livingstone, but I do know he is never seen with women. You must be pretty special to him for him to open up to you. He's a strong character around town and everyone looks up to him, but he seems to have his head screwed on. Do you really think he'd get mad over you going for a drink?"

Amelia shrugged.

"Toby, my ex, would have."

"Dash Livingstone is *not* Toby your ex," Jane said. "Dash Livingstone is a powerhouse, a Rockstar, a man who can have anything or anyone he wants…"

Amelia felt herself curl inwards.

"I don't know what happened exactly," Jane said as she reached out and touched Amelia gently on the arm. "But I thought at first, he sounded like a jerk, but when I thought about it and what you said, maybe it was just crossed wires. He didn't specifically say he wasn't happy about it, you just assumed he wasn't."

Amelia nodded.

"And you've just said you would kind of expect him to be because your ex was. I think by the sounds of it, you just need to talk and clear the air."

Amelia felt her guard go up again. She was not going to be approaching him. She hadn't heard from him for three days and she was getting more worked up by the minute.

"I think I just had to accept I'm not cut out for relationships," Amelia said. "I'm too damaged."

"You can be fixed," Jane said warmly. "And it seems to me like Dash was doing a pretty good job of that before this misunderstanding."

Jane was wise and she had calmed her down, Amelia had to admit that a lot of this made sense and she had to think on it. It was so hard for her to see either way, but she didn't know how he was truly feeling at this moment either.

She hugged Jane and thanked her, and then she made her way toward the door of the salon. It was time to go and collect Nora. It was time to be brave.

When Dash's last meeting of the day had ended, he sat at the conference table in the golf resort and looked out over the green. It may have been a slightly different view in that part of the meeting, but he couldn't help but think about the afternoon he had spent there with Amelia. Sitting in the club room and telling her about his little hometown, while also introducing him to his family.

It had been one of the happiest afternoons of his life. It had felt special to be showing her to them, for them to understand what it meant for her to be there and what had happened between them. And now he felt empty. As if she had left a hole and he was longing for it to be filled.

She had been so mad at him on the phone, and he knew now maybe he had been a good reason for that, but it hadn't been what he had intended. He wanted to make Amelia happy, and he had been foolish letting old hurts get into his head, while also reacting to the fact she was out there with Archer Savage, a goddam bear, and enemy of his family. But Amelia didn't know any of that. She was yet to be filled in properly. She only knew bits here and there, and she hadn't even seen Dash in his dragon form. He forgot how much she had had to absorb and take in since she had arrived in Misty Vale, and he had to be more understanding.

When Striker and Zane had asked him earlier how Amelia was and he had gone quiet, they had given each other a concerned look.

"She is something special," Zane had said. "Don't let the past ruin right now."

And he was right.

Dash had broken his phone after their conversation, and he had stewed all day Saturday and Sunday before only just getting a replacement that morning, and now so much time had passed he was feeling regretful. When he had seen that she hadn't been in touch with him, he knew that he had fucked up and he had to put it right.

Amelia was his woman, the one he was supposed to be with no matter what.

He rose to his feet and grabbed his papers and files before he stormed out of the board room and headed out of the golf club and to where the valet had parked his car near the front entrance. It was time for him to go and see his girls and explain himself once and for all.

* * *

As he turned into his street and saw the lights on inside the house, the chandelier twinkling brightly in the open glass pane that ran down the center of the building, he felt a rush of hope. He was hopeful that he wouldn't be too late, he was hopeful that the big bunch of red roses he had waiting on the seat next to him would show Amelia he had known how wrong he had been. But as he turned off the engine, he looked across at them and found himself scowling.

He didn't want to give her those. They were beautiful, but they were just flowers. He wanted to give her more than that.

When he opened the door and stepped inside, he felt the intensity of the silence and he knew that Nora already had to be in bed. His eyes scanned to the clock in the hallway and he saw that it was after seven, Amelia must have put her to bed early if she was super tired. He took a deep breath and walked slowly down the hall at the side of the house and into the kitchen and living area. The first thing he saw was Amelia, the way she was leaning over the island and her hair was falling down around her shoulders as she flipped through a magazine and looked so perfect it almost made his heart ache. To be close to her again, to feel her presence and to long for her made him want to kick himself all over. He really had been a fool, and now he had to try and explain himself.

She looked up slowly and their eyes met, and he could see the sadness behind them. He must have caused her a lot of pain over the past few days, and he would never forgive himself for it.

"Amelia," he said slowly as he stepped further into the room with his arms held out in surrender. "It is so good to see you."

She cocked her hair to the side, her expression not changing. She wasn't impressed with him and he knew it. When she still didn't speak, he rubbed his hand down his face and across his beard, the rough hairs scratching at his palm.

"Okay," he said honestly. "I know I've fucked up. And I'm sorry."

She still didn't change her expression. She really was steely, as if she had so much strength in her and was determined that she wouldn't bend. It was scaring him a little. In all his days he had never had a woman who challenged him so much, who stood up for herself and didn't just want him for his lifestyle and was willing to just let things slide to get their own way. Amelia was so different. It was no wonder his soul longed for hers, that his dragon craved her and imprinted on her the second their eyes met. He knew he couldn't live without her, and he had to show her.

"My past hasn't been easy," he said, knowing the only way was to lay it all out there. "Growing up in this town has been hard. Sure, Misty Vale may look as if it's perfect, but as you've heard from me and maybe even others around here, there is so much going on beneath the surface. To be born into a dragon shifter clan is pressure enough as it is. To also be a founding family of a town such as this, where there is so much history, so much mystery and paranormal activity, it hasn't been an easy ride. If you throw in what I've coped with in my life with Nora and my businesses and everything in between, I've had lot thrown at me. But nothing has ever phased me as much as you."

She uncrossed her arms, her resolve seeming to relax slightly.

"The other night, when you said you were heading out, I hold my hands up and admit I was a little bit worried because of what has happened to me in the past. But I didn't want to put that on you. It is my issue and I've worked through it in my head and I'm fine. I would never want to hold you back in life and I want you to know that. When you called and said you were in Archer's, I may have bristled slightly but only because of my past with the bears, of how things are with them even right now. There's a lot of bad feeling there, a lot of tension, which appears to be suddenly getting worse. But my anger wasn't with you, it was just with Archer. But I guess you know me so well, you must have picked up on it straight away and I'm sorry."

"It was very evident," she said, her shoulder sagging slightly as if she were relieved to hear all of this. "And even though I'm still mad, I want you to know that I know I over-reacted. In the past I've had shitty relationships and I've been controlled and lost all sense of myself. When I heard your tone change and I felt like you were being cold and distant, it felt like I was being punished and my walls went straight back up again."

"I would never want you to feel that way," Dash said taking a step closer. "It's the last thing I would ever want, or to make you feel."

She gave a weak smile.

"I think our pasts have both fucked us up a bit in the present," she said.

"You're telling me," Dash laughed, and he was relieved when Amelia laughed too.

"But that doesn't excuse you just blanking me and shutting me out for the past few days," she said. "After our conversation, I expected you to call."

"I know," he said with gritted teeth and a look of apprehension. "And again, this is my fault… I hurled my cell at the wall after you called me on Friday night, and it smashed completely."

She gave him a disapproving look.

"I only got a replacement today… but I didn't want to have this conversation over the phone… and over the weekend, I didn't want to come looking for you in case you didn't want to see me. You were pretty mad."

"I was," she smirked.

"I've been miserable," he admitted. "And I've thought about nothing but making it right with you."

She breathed out and he wanted to go to her. He wanted to hold her in his arms and reassure her that they would never be in this position again, that he was sorry, and that he wanted her to believe in him the way he believed in her.

"Amelia," Dash said as he took hold of her by the shoulders gently and looked at her dead in the eye. "I never want to be apart from you again. You have made me so insanely happy since you walked into my life, and Nora's. I love you Amelia. And I want you to know how much it not only takes for me to say that, but also that I am surer of it than anything I have ever known."

She smiled and he saw his fire in her eyes reflecting back into his. Touching her skin again, and holding her, was making him feel complete, and when he leaned in and kissed her she didn't resist, she opened her arms to him and wrapped them around his neck, letting him come to her and show her how much he did love her."

"I love you too," she breathed as their lips broke apart. "And I've been so down the past few days, so depressed at thinking we may never just be us again, that I even thought about leaving Misty Vale and never coming back."

"I'm so glad you didn't," he said as he traced his finger down the side of her face and brushed away a loose strand of hair. "Because I would have been lost without you."

He kissed her again and they held each other tightly.

Dash was so happy she had forgiven him, that she had explained her pain too, and that they were on track to make things right. But he still knew there was one more thing he had to do.

"Give me a moment," he said as he held up his finger and smiled. "There's something I want to show you."

Amelia looked at him with intrigue as he reached into his pocket and pulled out his cellphone. He pressed dial on a number and waited.

"Striker," he said, and Amelia seemed to furrow her brow as if this had not what she had been expecting. "I need you to do me a favor, could you come over to the house and sit here for a couple of hours? There's something I need to do."

· · ·

WHEN STRIKER ARRIVED FROM HIS OWN HOME TWO DOORS down, Amelia looked even more confused as Dash took her hand in his and led her toward the back doors of the kitchen that led out into the garden.

They stood in the cold night air, the stars above them vast and heavy, their little lights twinkling and the moon bright and sharp in a perfect crescent sitting proudly above the pines.

"What are we doing?" she asked breathlessly, as if the cold were getting to her.

"Don't worry," he said. "You won't feel it in a minute."

She half laughed and shrugged as if she was going to roll with it and then Dash looked back over his shoulder and into the kitchen.

"Striker will sit for as long as we need and keep an eye on Nora," he said. "Because there's something you need to see…"

CHAPTER 17

*A*melia's nerves were starting to get the better of her as she stood out in the garden with Dash, her heart and mind racing at what may be about to happen.

She gripped his hand and he squeezed it reassuringly as they began to walk away from the house and out into the pine forest. They walked and walked, and the trees were so dense and thick that the sky above them seemed to disappear every few moments, until they finally reached a clearing, and it came back fully into view. Amelia looked around, and she could tell that this place was somewhere that Dash came often. It was a perfect circle in the center of the forest, some-where completely shut off from the outside world. On either side of them there wasn't anything to be seen except the trees and the forest, and above them there was only sky.

"What is this place?" she asked. "It's lovely."

She could see that in the very center there was a circle of stones and the remnants of a fire that had long burned out, but the ash that was present did suggest it had maybe been alight even just days before. She saw big logs, trunks of fallen trees, had been arranged around the stone circle, as if maybe they had been used as seating, but they were so big and as they moved toward them she ran her hands along them and felt the soft bark.

"This is somewhere my pack and I come," he said. "We come here to shift."

"To shift?" she looked up at him and felt her heart beat a little harder.

Dash nodded and squeezed her hand again. She could tell that he didn't want her to be nervous, but at the same time, that was going to be almost impossible. She was still getting her head around all of this, and even though she could feel the dragon within him, and she felt the power and energy flow through her, she was also unsure of what would happen when she actually saw Dash turn into this majestic beast. It was both exciting and terrifying, but she knew that she had to experience to know him fully. She had to see how it happened, what it did to him, how she felt with the dragon before she could give herself to Dash properly and let him claim her for the rest of time.

"Okay," she whispered. "I'm ready."

He hadn't had to ask her, and she didn't want to talk about the subject for a long time. She wanted to throw herself in headfirst and see what was about to happen.

"Are you sure?" Dash asked.

"Very," she smiled and nodded with reassurance for him. "I want and need to know this side of you."

Dash nodded too and then he slowly dropped her hand as he stepped back and moved into the center of the clearing so he was as far from Amelia as he could be without getting too close to the trees. She found herself stepping back and moving to the other side of one of the fallen logs. She was afraid, but she was also at peace with the whole thing. She had to see him now, she had to understand him and the inner workings of his world.

Dash had been right, the cold in the clearing seemed to be nonexistent, as if it had dragon energy all over and around in. The ground even seemed to feel warm and her skin was no longer cold. She looked ahead and found Dash's eyes. She stared into them deeply as she watched him slowly removing his clothes. He kicked off his boots, then his jeans, before he pulled his sweater, then t-shirt off over his head and stood there looking like an absolute god. The moonlight seemed to light up the tattoo on his chest, one of a great dragon, and it made her swoon. His muscles were so taught, and he was so powerful, that as he stood there almost completely naked, she bit her lip and tried not to let her lust for him overpower her.

Suddenly, the air around them seemed to change and it took her by surprise. She stepped back instinctively and gasped as she saw Dash's whole frame begin to move and warp. She heard the screams and roars escape from his lips before he began to change. His arms and legs grew longer, his whole body almost tripled in size before his skin split open and scales came in its place. A dragon began to form before her very eyes, and Amelia's mouth sagged open as once the dragon was fully there it began to edge closer and closer to the tips of the trees as its size increased again.

"My God," she gasped.

She could feel Dash's heat and as the dragon looked down at her she saw his eyes there, he was still inside, and it made her nerves quieten slightly.

The dragon lowered its head, and she took a nervous step closer. He was so big and powerful, and as she reached out and stroked its scales she jumped back slightly as she felt the heat pulsing away beneath the scales.

"Wow," she said with a smile as she looked into his eyes.

The dragon nudged her slightly and at first, she didn't know what he meant, but when she realized he wanted her to try and climb up onto his back she almost couldn't believe it.

"You want me to climb on?" she asked.

The dragon nudged her toward the log with its long nose and she climbed up onto that first before she reached out and heaved herself up onto the scales and held on tight.

"Oh my," she whispered.

She didn't know what was going to happen, but when the dragon pushed off the ground and launched them both into the air, she closed her eyes tight and barely dared breathe. She didn't know how she wasn't falling off, but something inside of her just knew exactly how and where to hold onto him, and as she gained the nerves to open her eyes and look, she saw that they were soaring over the mountains of Misty Vale and it was like no other view she had ever seen.

"This is amazing," she tried to call to him, but she was unsure whether he had heard because of the wind whipping past them as Dash gained speed.

She gripped onto him tightly, and as they swooped through the night sky it felt as if she could reach out and touch the stars. The little lights of the town below only made her feel warmer inside, and as they began to descend back down toward the clearing, Amelia had never felt so exhilarated before. It truly had been the most incredible experience.

The dragon touched down onto the warm ground, his scales exuding even more heat. Amelia felt it radiating into her hands, and her whole body felt hot, as if she were absorbing the dragon's energy. She waited for him to move over toward the log and when she managed to swing her legs over and slip down onto it, she turned and looked back into his eyes.

"That was truly incredible Dash," she said as she rested her head against the dragon's nose. "Thank you."

The dragon paused for a moment before he moved backwards, and she braced herself for what was about to come. She saw his shoulders heaving, its enormous belly moving in and out quickly as if it were gearing up to do a tremendous roar. When it came she covered her ears and closed her eyes for a split second, before she opened them again to see the dragon spurt fire into the stone circle in the center of the forest and it caught light in just the right place, making the whole clearing appear in red and orange glows.

She smiled and watched in awe, as within a few moments the dragons frame began to shake and shrink. The scales gave way to skin and slowly but surely Dash began to take shape again before her very eyes.

She was breathless and panting, and when he had fully transformed back into his human self, they ran to each other and she let herself be wrapped up in his red-hot embrace. His skin was on fire, but it didn't faze her, his skin was so hot it should have made her flinch, but she had the dragon's energy inside of her now too, she had taken it into herself and now she could hold him and feel the immense power coming from way deep inside of him.

She looked at his tattoo properly, and the flames of the fire in the stone circle seemed to catch on the outline of it and made it glimmer and shine, as if it were alive with magical ink.

"This," she said as she reached up and traced her finger around the outline. "It's you?"

Dash nodded, still breathless himself from his transformation but with a fire and lust in his eyes that Amelia knew would not be tamed. She felt it too, her whole body was turned on and desperate for him. Her nipples were hard, her pussy was wet, and she bit her lip as she wrapped her arms around his neck and let him lift her up so that her legs were wrapped around his waist.

He walked with her across the cleaning, out of the path of the dragon fire and toward a more secluded spot where there were pine branches laying across the soft, moist earth. When he lay her down and kneeled back, she looked up at him in all his glory, at the glimmering ink on his chest, alive with fire, at the flames in his eyes and the heat coming from his body. This man was everything. He was so strong and powerful, so frightening, and everything she had never knew she needed.

She lay back and offered herself to him. There had never been a moment more perfect than this, and she knew that there was no going back. Amelia wanted Dash to claim her. She wanted to be with him for the rest of time as his one true and fated mate. She wanted him to love and protect her, she wanted to experience it all.

He took hold of her leg with his big, hot hands and moved up to her waist where he began to slowly unbutton her jeans. She lay there, completely at his mercy, as he slid them down her thighs, over her knees and off the end of her feet. When he reached for her top it came off quickly, then her bra with a swift snap. She gasped and smiled, her eyes alive with his energy, and when he slipped his fingers into the corners of her panties and yanked them down, she moaned with pleasure.

She had thought about this moment so many times. She knew how skilled he was in the bedroom, he had shown her night after night when he had pleasured her, but she had never yet felt him. Never taken his immense power... and now the time had come.

He was so hard, so big and engorged. And when he came toward her and put his weight on her she held her breath as she prepared for him to enter her. He raised her leg slightly, gripping her thigh with his hand, while with his other he guided himself into her, just a little at first, which almost tipped her over the edge, but then his full length, which made her entire body quiver with pleasure.

She threw her head back, her whole body bucking and shuddering as he thrust into her slowly over and over again. Dash pinned her down into the soft, pure earth, his tensed thighs guiding hers open even deeper, letting him reach places she didn't even know were there.

She looked up into his eyes as he bore down on her, and she ran her hands through his hair, they were so locked in on each other, that when they both began to come at the exact same time, she felt something even deeper transfer between them. A fire and an energy that could not be compared to anything else. Something so powerful and raw that it made them both scream aloud with sheer delight. Her orgasm tore through her as he spilled his seed, and the fire in both of their eyes ignited and continued to burn. The heat was overpowering, and when Dash finally collapsed on top of her, Amelia was so exhausted and quivering, she could barely make sense of what had just happened.

She tried to open her eyes, but she was seeing stars and fire, a warm sensation was spreading through her veins, overpowering her, and making her feel more alive than ever. More so than the first night in Dash's bed. She knew she had a piece of him inside of her forever. He had given her some of his power, she had been claimed by the dragon.

"Amelia," he panted as he held onto her and ran his hands through her hair, staring deep into her eyes before he kissed her longingly and lovingly.

"That was…" she couldn't even find the words.

He smiled and kissed her again.

When they found that they could rise to their feet, Dash held her hand as they collected their clothes, dressed each other, and began to walk back to the house hand in hand. Amelia felt as if she were seeing the world differently, as if she were experiencing life for the first time. Magic was present in the forest, she felt it. She could sense the change in the air, the mystical creatures hiding in the shadows. And she knew that she had found the place that she was supposed to be, somewhere she could be herself and grow with her man by her side.

When they reached Dash's home and went inside Striker took one look at them and seemed to know what happened. He smiled and crossed the room and embraced his brother, before he did the same with Amelia and looked at her, the fire in both their eyes catching each other's. She hadn't been able to see it before with Striker and Zane, but now she had been claimed it appeared that she would be able to see it now in all other dragons, to help her recognize their kind. And it felt amazing.

"Welcome to the family, Amelia," Striker said with a knowing smile before he wished them goodnight and left them to enjoy each other again.

Up in bed, Amelia and Dash held each other, looking deep into each other's eyes, the fire roaring gently in the background, the stars of the heavens and the moon shining in through the French doors, and she had never felt more happy or content than this.

"I'm yours Dash," she whispered. "Forever."

He smiled and nodded, them both knowing that something life changing had happened between them in the forest, deep in the mountains of Misty Vale.

They had given themselves to each other. And now they were both home.

our Weeks Later

THE SCHOOL BELL RANG RIGHT ON TIME, AND AS AMELIA waited underneath the beautiful red and orange of the old maple tree she smiled as she realized fall had well and truly come to Misty Vale.

The colors were so rich and intense, she was sure she had never believed that such beauty could truly exist, and yet here she was, experiencing it firsthand.

When the doors to school opened and Nora came running down the steps, Amelia raised her hand to wave as Nora's little eyes searched for her to find her in the crowd.

When she bounded over, Amelia scooped her up and gave her a big cuddle and a kiss on the cheek.

"Hey little lady," she beamed and said in her best British accent. "And how was your day dear?"

Nora burst out laughing and nuzzled into her again

before Amelia set her down on the ground. She grinned up at her and held onto her hand.

"It was wonderful thank you Mary Poppins," she said with a laugh. "Today we learned all about volcanos… and oh my goodness, they are so cool! Have you ever seen one?"

Amelia smiled.

"I've seen them on TV and in pictures," Amelia said. "But never in real life."

Nora was so sweet and innocent, and it was crazy to think that even though she was descended from a dragon, that she had no idea what her father truly was. That he had fire and heat running through him just like a volcano did. Amelia couldn't help but wonder when the time would come for Dash to sit her down and tell her all about her family history, or whether in fact Nora could even develop some shifting powers of her own as she grew into a young woman and hit her teens.

"I love them, even more than the planets," Nora said with a wide smile. "I love the fiery stuff in them."

"The lava?" Amelia asked.

"That's it!" Nora said excitedly. "It's awesome!"

Amelia smiled, Nora was clearly drawn to heat and fire.

As they walked away from school hand in hand and went on their way down Main Street, Amelia looked at all the stores and faces that were all becoming so familiar to her now. She had been in Misty Vale for almost seven weeks, and she had truly found a place to call home. She had never once looked back and missed the coast, or her old life there. She had fallen into small town mountain life and embraced it as her own. She had found something special there in this mystical spot, and now as she began the newest chapter of her life as the wife of a dragon, the claimed fated mate, she was happier than she had ever been.

They walked past Jane's and Amelia waved in at truly the

best friend she had ever made, and Jane came jogging toward the door and opened it wide.

"Hey girls," Jane grinned. "How are you both doing today?"

"Awesome," Nora said. It appeared that *awesome* was the word of the day.

"Well that sure is good to hear," Jane smiled. "Have you seen that the Oktoberfest is coming along? Town is going to be packed!"

"Dash and I were just saying this morning that it's not long now," Amelia nodded. "Looks like there's going to be lots of people heading into town from this weekend, I guess we all better be prepared!"

"Oh, it'll be plenty of fun, I'm sure," Jane said with a raised brow. "Good for business anyway."

"Very true," Amelia laughed. "We should all get together on Saturday night and head out to it, I'm sure Dash and I can get a sitter."

"Fantastic," said Jane. "I'll keep the diary clear."

The girls said goodbye to each other, and Amelia and Nora started walking again, they passed by lots of places setting up for the biggest event of the Autumn calendar in Misty Vale, and it was guaranteed to be a hectic albeit festive weekend.

They rounded another corner and Dash's office came into view, Nora ran ahead slightly and peered through the window, looking for her father and Amelia's heart felt so full as she saw the little girl's face light up as she clearly saw him inside. These were the moments that made a life, she thought. This is what it is all about.

Dash opened the office doors and he picked up Nora, as she wrapped her arms around his neck and pressed her cheek against his, so they could both smile back at Amelia.

It was so strange to think she had come to Misty Vale

completely on her own, with a broken heart and no idea of how things would turn out. And now, even just a short time later, she had found something some never do… she had found a family. She had found a husband and a daughter, and they were moving forward in life together and loving each other in such a wonderful way it was just perfect.

Nora ran off inside to say hello to some of the other people in the office, and Dash came to Amelia, looked into her eyes and she saw his fire there, which always made her feel as if she had come home. He kissed her lovingly on the lips, and then they entwined their fingers together, once again ready to take on the world.

"So," Dash said with a knowing smile. "I guess it's time for dancing and then dinner?"

"It sure is," Amelia replied.

Nora joined them back out on the street, and they all walked away together. Since Amelia was no longer the nanny but Nora's stepmom, they dedicated one night a week where Dash would leave work early and join the girls as they took Nora to dance class and then headed to their favorite restaurant on Main Street… the cute little bistro that Dash had seen Amelia in on her first week in town. It had been like their first date, and it was tradition now that they always went there once a week and ordered three plates of the spaghetti marinara. It was their place now, the three of them.

As they walked along the streets of Misty Vale together, Amelia looked at them both and smiled. Her stepdaughter and her dragon… fate had brought them together, and now, they were joined for the rest of time.

Things had never been so perfect, and she had never been so happy… the fire inside her burned bright for their future and all that was to come.

* * *

Thank you so much for reading Dragon Daddy's Nanny! We hope you enjoyed the first story in the Misty Vale series! If you enjoyed it then we think you will want to read the rest of Samantha's Series!

Click here to get the newly released Lone Reach Shifters Box Set!

Of course we have a preview for you too…

The cold gripped them as Chloe grabbed as many of their things as she could and shoved them in the bags waiting on the bed. The icy air from outside seemed to be filtering into the house, turning the place to stone and making their teeth chatter. Chloe knew she didn't have a lot of time, and Harper was watching her mother with wide eyes, fully aware something was happening, even though Chloe was doing her best to disguise it.

She moved quickly, but kept calm, she smiled down at her daughter as she zipped up the bags and slung them over her shoulder before she reached for the little girl's hand and pulled her gently to her feet.

"Come on then, kiddo," she said with as much cheerfulness as she could muster. "It's time for us to go on a little adventure."

Harper held her soft, worn toy bunny close to her chest and nodded her head as she and her mom made for the door and down the stairs of their home. Chloe had to keep her face straight and the quiver out of her voice. She had to move fast and get them the hell out of Bridge Hollow while she still had the chance.

They stepped out into the frigid temps, the cold nipping their skin, and the moon shining brightly in the sky overhead as they slipped down the driveway, clutching to each other and trying to keep their balance, toward the car.

When Chloe loaded Harper into the back and fastened her seat belt, she smiled down at her little girl and kissed her on the forehead.

So much had happened in the past year, and now, she was ready to make a fresh start for them both. This was their chance to begin again.

Some may have called it running away, but for Chloe, it was just the necessary step she had to take to move on with her life and keep her and her daughter safe.

She climbed in the driver's seat and adjusted the rearview mirror before she started the engine.

The whole town felt eerily quiet, and the chaos of the past few months had calmed almost overnight, but still, she knew she couldn't stay there.

What if he ever came back?

She shuddered at the thought and pressed the gas, gripping the wheel and steering them swiftly off into the night.

Chloe may have been leaving Bridge Hollow – a place she had always called home – but she was doing what was right.

And now, there was no turning back.

The roads seemed to thaw the further away she traveled, and as she wound through the mountain roads, rising high and dipping into the trees, again and again, she began to get the sensation back in her fingers. She had felt as if she had spent the best part of six months frozen to the bone, but now that she was putting distance between herself and that place, she was finally coming back into the land of the living.

The distance between Bridge Hollow would be a shield for her against all the bad that had happened… and, of course, him.

As long as he didn't know where they were, they were safe.

She flashed her eyes up to the rearview mirror and checked on Harper. She was fast asleep, cuddled in a fluffy blanket with a pillow under her head. They had been on the road a couple of hours, but she had been asleep within twenty minutes and hadn't stirred since.

Chloe smiled warmly and then cast her glance back to the winding mountain road ahead. She had done the right thing. And now, she was on her way to a new place to start a new life… wherever that may be…

She yawned and blinked, trying to keep herself awake. It had been one hell of a day and night, and now, as it was nearing 4am, she had no idea how she was going to keep driving.

She gripped the wheel and sat forward, trying to focus, and as she turned another bend and started out on another sharp edge of the mountain highway, she felt the nerves creep along her spine.

"I hope there's a motel somewhere near here," she whispered to herself, even though she didn't truly hold out much hope.

She had lived in Bridge Hollow her entire life, but she had rarely left, and when she had, she had always driven toward warmer climates, never further into the mountain range like this. Had she made a mistake coming to unchartered territory? Should she have just gone toward the West and found a city to get lost in?

She shook her head.

Chloe was a small-town girl and the thought of ending up in a city was overwhelming. She needed somewhere quiet and unassuming… somewhere no one would ever think to look.

The snow may have stopped falling, and the harsh cold of Bridge Hollow may not be reaching her, but she could tell Mother Nature was still wanting to play. It was the bleakest of midwinter, and she was driving through mountains she didn't know, in the middle of the night, with her child in the back seat, sleeping soundly. Suddenly, the gravity of her situation started to hit her, and she felt tears prick the corner of her eyes.

How had she gotten herself into this mess?

She reached up and wiped the tears away. Determined not to dwell on what had happened to her over the past year, and even more certain she didn't want to give *him* any more of her head space. Her thoughts were swirling like the darkness ahead of her and she blinked as she realized it had started to snow again. The small flakes were flying at the windshield, making her feel as if she were in a spinning tunnel, and she was becoming dizzy.

She gripped the wheel and sat forward, pressing the breaks slowly to avoid skidding, and to make sure she didn't become too disorientated in the mix of darkness and snowflakes being caught by her headlights.

She felt a rumble underneath her, and for a split second, she thought there was a problem with the car. She clenched her teeth and pressed the breaks again, willing the car to stop comfortably as to not wake Harper, but as soon as the motion stilled, she became aware that the rumble was not from the engine but from something further away.

She felt her mouth gape open as she squinted out into the night. She couldn't see a whole lot, but she could tell that both sides of the road were steep slopes running up into the mountains, as if the road had been built right through the middle of one. She bit her lip and held her breath, trying not to make a sound.

The rumble thundered again, and behind her, she was aware of Harper stirring and her little voice calling, "Mom?" before, without warning, their vehicle was pushed forward, a huge rush of snow powering into them from behind.

Chloe tried her best not to scream but was unsuccessful. Out of instinct, she reached her hand into the back seat to grab hold of Harper, trying to protect her in any way that she could…

GET YOUR COPY OF THE LONE REACH SHIFTERS ON AMAZON here!